I'm a pe_ _ _ _ _ _ _....
..but in a fun way!

Written by
Blake Robson

x Stating the oblivious x

Gravel doesn't taste very nice. And neither do my mother's nipples.
I am sitting in a standard Turkish greasy spoon café. The Rose Café to be precise. The café is situated in Haringey, London, has bloody awful oxblood coloured metal chairs paired with a white and red plastic table. I'm very particular about furniture. I don't mind if it's cheap crap but even cheap crap can be palatable. These seats are not only shite, they are uncomfortable and not suitable for the job they were supposed to fulfil, which is a fairly simple one. To be sat on! That's it! How difficult can that be?
I am 29 years of age and am supposedly a man (you know when you hear on the news that a 20 year old 'man' has committed man slaughter due to a fight outside some trashy middle England nightclub at 2am and the unfortunate fella on the receiving end of his fist has hit his head on a curb and died and I think, 'A man? 20 years old! A man!' Jesus, he's not a man. I'm 29 and I still don't consider myself to be one. Surely he's still a child even though at sixteen you can legally fuck, get married, join the army and kill foreigners, but you're still not allowed a goddamned pint in a pub. A man indeed!
I am of slight but muscular build and in reasonably good shape due to having weight trained since I was 16. Though with no real intensity, I had enough vanity and ego to keep me training all these years and also, it gives you a bit more confidence that you can defend yourself if you must. I am quite

heavily tattooed on my arms, body, neck, hands, and I have a small inverted cross below my left eye. The tattoos are mostly of an old school, nautical origin. I like cliché tattoos. I am 5'8 but probably actually 5'7 1/2 if I was being honest (I wear boots a lot). I hate being this height, but with no overpowering complex to speak of, though I do long to be 5'10. Given that I am sitting in a café for the 3rd time this weekend, you can assume that my diet, however, is quite terrible along with the smoking, heavy drinking and the occasional drugs I like to put inside myself. I have long curly hair and often am told I look like Russell Brand (definitely not), Jack Sparrow (no way), Heath Ledger or Gary Oldman (possibly). I do look a bit piratey, but I don't own a ship. Like a dick without balls: all show. My skin complexion is vampiric. I despise those dull, unimaginative tossers that fly all the way to Egypt or South America and just sit around the swimming pool, turning themselves into leather as though the most important thing in the world is to be brown. Usually these are often the very people that vote UKIP and hate brown people. My attire consists of blue turned-up heavy jeans, heavy reddish dark brown leather Red Wing boots a plain grey marl t-shirt and a vintage faded blue Levis denim jacket that is a bit to small for me. On my lapel is a small badge of a bird that my Swedish friend Sara gave to me.

Sitting alone after a run around the local park I am enjoying a fry-up however I am being distracted by a fat white woman with her two, loud, mixed-race 3-year-old children sitting in a cheap plastic blue dirty pram. Whilst eating a mix of bacon,

black pudding, egg and beans - a small component of each stuffed onto an aged, not terribly clean metal fork - I am reading a rather wonderful book called Atomised or 'Les Particules Elementaries,' which is the original French title.
I am towards the end of this book at a rather sad and moving section. At this juncture, the point is raised retrospectively, that these characters might have had or could still have children and that that could possibly make them happy. Could it give them some purpose? This is something I have often pondered but in no great seriousness due to my being perpetually single. Whilst reading I wonder once more, should I have children some day? People do seem to adore them (not the fat white woman though) despite the endless hassle it brings to their lives. I often wonder if they are being truthful. It's surely one of the worst social things a person can admit. To announce that they do in fact regret having children, and that those ungrateful brats have ruined their lives. I am beginning to consider that maybe I should have children, whilst at the very same time I'm saying to myself quite vacantly in relation to the two winging shit-bags, 'Why don't they shut their little fucking mouth holes,' and somehow not actually realising that I was having these vicious thoughts whilst simultaneously contemplating the love of a child. That was until I caught myself doing it of course. The fat woman in the tracksuit bottoms (that have never seen a track or the inside of any kind of a gym) and her two whining, nipple-suckers leave at last and I get some peace. I continue to read.

At this point in the book, life seems to be incredibly vacuous, desperate, and almost if not certainly, pointless. The woman, who is only 40, who was very beautiful had never found love or had had children. On finding out she had become pregnant with her childhood friend she at last felt happy. Soon after discovering her pregnancy she was diagnosed with cervical cancer and was told it would be better to abort the child.
The woman, Annabelle, then creeps out of her partner's bed and takes an overdose on the sofa and leaves a note reading 'I have decided to die, surrounded by those who love me.'

Annabelle's following cremation naturally reminds me of my own father's cremation a few months earlier. I notice that my eyes are beginning to well and tears are forming more rapidly than I can control. Luckily the café is almost empty and no one notices so I surreptitiously slip on my sunglasses to hide my reddening wet eyes. I close the book, look out the window at a used car parts shop and compose myself. I hope this book has a happy ending.

x Genocidal pea flickers x

On the following Thursday, whilst eating my dinner alone in a Chinese restaurant named 'Wok You Like', I notice a child choosing to eat peas.
When my sister and I were kids we used to flick peas behind a giant slab of a freezer. It's one of those from the 80's that you lift the lid open like a car boot. They are ideal for a whole year's worth of meat or at least 3 dead bodies. We flicked the said peas because our oppressors (mum and dad, mostly dad) would not let us leave the table until we had finished all of our food. A concept I still believe today to be ridiculous. I didn't like peas when I was a child and I still don't like the green bastards now (not racist). To be fair to peas they were not the only food I detested. Most vegetables can include themselves in this category. Carrots, they can fuck off (apart from carrot cake… Mmmm). Mushrooms, (a fungus) they are the worst of all, they are squidgy snail's excrement and there's even one called Shit-ache.
So what did you achieve by force-feeding us those disgusting beasts? If anything, perhaps that is why I still hate them (I can't speak for my sister). It's not as though we were going to grow up and say, I don't eat food because my parents didn't force me to when I was a kid. I'm going to survive on air & dick milk.

x Women leave toothbrushes in bathrooms like dogs
piss on trees x

On the following Friday night after a few
hours of our date (if you can call it that)
at the Salisbury pub on Green Lanes, a girl
of Turkish descent but really a Londoner who
says to me, 'I'm Turkish, I'm Turkish' even
though she was born in England and has lived
here her entire life. In that case I'm
Mongolian. Welsh people do that. I dated a
girl who was even born and raised in England
and couldn't be more English. Just because
her parents were Welsh she claimed she was,
and when the rugby was on she supported
Wales over England.
Adele, the 'Turkish' girl, comes over to my
place semi-regularly and we have regular
sex. She is very pretty, she has a great
figure and nice little brown nipples but is
not relaxed enough in her brain to be able
to cum, or perhaps it's my fault. She says
it isn't. Don't they all say that? She says
she has never cum before. She said the last
guy she dated was too nice and she needed
someone to take control in the bedroom
because she doesn't really know what she's
doing. I normally don't like it if girls
can't cum and this is no exception but she
is very pretty and uncommonly for me I just
selfishly fuck her how I want to fuck her to
make myself cum, I'm bored of trying to make
her orgasm. It's a bit like porn fucking but
slightly more respectful and a few less
cameras and cum shots in the face. When I do
cum I feel mildly satisfied and a bit guilty
at the same time and she seems happy enough
with the event. I pour another gin and tonic
and roll another cigarette. I don't care how

cliché smoking a cigarette after screwing is it's truly marvellous.
Women do leave toothbrushes in bathrooms like dogs piss on trees. They do it accidentally on purpose so that they can a) come back because they've left an item they forgot and b) to warn off any other bitches. Does having sex with a lot people make you a bad person? I don't see why it should. I just want to fuck everyone. Well not everyone but you know what I mean. I can't help it. Variety is the joy of the unknown and excitement of anticipation. Every single woman is completely different in bed which can be a pain in the neck in some ways but also magical. As long as you're not a complete arsehole to women and they know where they stand then there's no harm, as long as you're honest with people. I have slept with just short of 100 people. 86 to be exact. When I say people, I mean women. Men and children have never been an interest to me although I did snog a male friend when I was 21 when we were in a shitty city club in Leicester and it was the first time we took ecstasy and left our safe little village. I've slept with women from New Zealand, Australia, South Africa, Germany, Jersey, Wales and England, of course. The USA, Canada, Venezuela, Norway, Hungary, Czech, Poland, Italy, France, China, Russia, Turkey, Mauritius, Spain, Portugal, Italy, Brazil, China and Denmark but there's still so many countries to visit. It makes my brain hurt thinking about all the women I can't or won't ever have sex with. I might be ill. I once fucked a real fatty. I met her on Tinder and when she turned up I thought, 'For fuck's sake!' but after 6 pints I thought well I'm not doing anything else tonight, and her tits were just so

massive I thought I've never seen tits this big and they didn't look too saggy, 'Fuck it,' I thought, 'Why not.' I was rewarded when I unleashed those beasts. When they flopped out of her bra they expanded even more and just about filled the entire room. It was tit-tastic! I played with them like a kitten plays with a giant cotton wool ball just pawing at them and staring wide-eyed at the enormity of the fucking things. I went down on her for some reason, maybe because I knew I was just going to fuck her really hard whilst staring at her massive, massive tits and thought it was only fair. Sometimes I think that I try too hard to please the person I'm sleeping with rather than just enjoying it, or at least I have been told that once. It can be difficult to strike the right balance. I put her on her back and got to it. Then I turned her over, which wasn't the best sight as her arse was massive but it was dark so it was okay. I reached around and I couldn't even get her whole tit in my hand and it weighed about the same as a small child. I turned her on her back again as I decided I really wanted a full frontal view and in no time I filled her up. Filled her up might be bragging a bit. My payload really isn't that substantial. To my dismay when I went to the bathroom I turned the light on and looked in the mirror and I had a red ring of blood around my mouth that looked like I had been feasting on a fucking corpse, night of the living dead style. I nearly threw up. Dirty bitch must have known she had the painters in!

It has become a slight fixation of mine to get to a grand total of sleeping with 100 different women. I don't think it's because I want to brag about it. I never discuss my sex life with other people. In fact if it's a current affair, I'm dead against it. That's personal stuff not for sharing though I'm well aware that women like to discuss their encounters in detail. I think it's damn rude. It's not for other people's ears. If enough time has passed, or you don't know the person, then I don't mind that, but not when you're sitting opposite some guy and the day before you were informed by his girlfriend that he liked being wanked off by feet (it's called frogging). Give the man some privacy.

My obsession may just be boyish immaturity or maybe it's just because it's so much fucking fun and people like to set themselves targets. It gives you something to aim for. Perhaps I am ashamed of my behaviour or maybe not. Should I be? Maybe when I reach 100, I will eventually meet someone and fall in love. I do long to fall in love, "Every man needs a companion, I know I do". I certainly don't want to be in my 40s chasing women around like some dirty old paedophile. I'd like to age with a bit of moral fibre and dignity.
Perhaps I didn't get enough attention as a teenager or I wasn't the coolest kid. I would say I was on the periphery of the cool gang though never at the centre of it and I had my fair share of girls but you always feel inadequate at school. I do find that even now I still get incredibly envious of others kissing in clubs, or hear people fucking next door even if I am myself am fucking or kissing someone at the very same time. Silly business really!
I also suffer from a condition known as Sexomnia. When you explain it to people, especially women before you go to bed with

them and you've agreed just to sleep, they look at you like, 'yeah right, that's a good one!' The nuts and bolts of Sexomnia is that I am capable of having full-blown sex with someone whilst I'm fast asleep and not know a damn thing about it. Sometimes I wake up half way through and go, 'Oh! I'm having sex. Er… right. I'll just carry on then, shall I?'

When you describe it to people it sounds more like night rape but I'm easily deterred and not forceful I'm told. That's what I'd tell the judge anyway. I was informed by a woman I spent the night with, that I was fucking her from behind in the middle of the night and then just suddenly stopped in the middle of it and said to her 'Sleep!'

A recent revelation from someone else I briefly dated was that after the first time we'd had sex during the night I proceeded to fuck her every hour on the hour. She told me I screwed her around seven times in the night. She said that she was incredibly tired and she was getting sore and I didn't know a damn thing about it, which is a shame because it sounded great. I couldn't achieve that in my waking hours. I asked her why she didn't stop me and she said she just thought I was just very eager and I hadn't told her about my condition so I suppose she wouldn't have known but she must have thought I was a sex maniac.

The problem started when I was with my beloved Xan and she told me that she liked it because she said 'it was like having sex with a stranger'. I'm not sure if that's a good thing? Another girl I was having casual sex with told me that in the middle of the night I went down on her and then licked her anus! I hope she'd cleaned it! It would be fair to say it's true that I do sometimes objectify women. I put them in two camps. The ones I want to fuck and then the ones I don't. Of course, that is not the whole truth. It's just an immediate response I have when I see a girl/woman/lady. A bit like how we all judge people the second we meet them, although I have a feeling that I may be more judgemental than most. It's difficult to know as you can't climb inside other people's brain holes, and people keep this stuff to themselves so people don't run away. To clarify, when I say I put women into two camps that's not how I judge them if I would like to befriend or spend time with them. It's just an instinctive response I get in the first 2 seconds, ingrained within us via our ancestors, resulting from the task of searching for a mate. Is that normal, does everyone do this? I certainly don't think of women as anything less than a man's equal or more than likely they are superior to men. I just like having sex with them. A lot! I hope and fantasise that women are better than men, at least morally. Men have had their chance at shaping this world and have done a damn fine job of royally fucking it up. Murder, genocide, war, mind control, religion, forced marriage, bogus cults, football hooligans, homophobia, sexism, estate agents, lederhosen, female genital mutilation and legal rape, but to name a few. I would hazard to say that men have committed 99% of all the crimes against humanity and Mother Earth! This all because of men's evolutionary and original physical position of power over women, so women never really had a chance and even today there are barbaric and antiquated behaviours, attitudes and rituals that are still taking place right this very second that mistreat women. I would like to think that if it had been the other way around and women ruled the world, it would be a kinder, more giving and empathetic one, surely it couldn't be any worse than the one we're living in now? Who knows, perhaps all people in power cannot be relied upon not to exert cruelty on those below them that do not adhere to their ideals. Maybe men would have been treated as nothing more than sperm carriers and for that use alone, just like women have been. I have always thought that women probably are better than men, however browsing through Tinder I'm really not so sure. I would say 80% of the women on there are superficial, uninteresting, narcissistic Barbie dolls where every photo on their Instagram is of their OWN FACE! Just having a face that looks nice is NOT AN ACHIEVEMENT!!!

I suspect, however, this problem is probably man's fault as they objectified women in the first place. It's hardly any wonder they have become objects. Imagine about a million Kim Kardashian clones (Star Wars pun coming: 'Attack Of The Clowns'). That's pretty much what is to be found on Tinder. An army of fuckpigs covered in too much make up with fake tits, injected lips and as much personality as a stick! The problem is, deep down I still want to fuck them but that's all, I almost enjoy degrading them as they have done to themselves! I'm informed there are just as many if not more men on the other side with photos of their six packs and cocks out. I suppose these retards will pair up and they get what they deserve. The woman dating a guy who fancies himself more than her and him having to take staged photos of her when they're on the beach and when the evening arrives and they are sat down to dinner and all they've got is their

stupid faces and nothing to say. Another
photo?

x Pipe hugging x

I'm not completely sure when I made the decision to act in such a way that ignores consequences. Perhaps ignoring isn't the correct word. I didn't ignore them. I knew there would be consequences. Maybe it's more that I just didn't care anymore. Somewhere along the line I lost what I once thought life meant, not that I ever really knew but at least I had my suspicions. It may have been when - come to think of it, yes I think this *was* then. I had been out all day drinking for someone's 30th birthday, which was not the best time for a revelation admittedly. It was a relatively dull affair where the girl/woman (what's the definition exactly?), whose birthday it was, received whilst I was in attendance a Gucci hand bag. The recipient screamed and flapped her hands in utter delight like someone had just told her she had been nominated the new queen of the carnival. The bag cost a total of £2,000. Yes, you read it right. Two thousand pounds! I'm not sure that there's a greater symbolism of what's wrong with the world. Her loving family and boyfriend bought the bag for this girl. He is my mate, as it happens, although at this point I am beginning to wonder why and what the hell do we actually have in common. You could travel half way around the world, buy a motorbike, a full-on Storm Trooper outfit! Give it to me. I'll make the most of it. Anything's better than a fucking handbag! Imagine how much Pick N Mix you could buy!!
After about 10 hours of drinking which is the only way I'm sure this random collection of friends and family can even tolerate each other, I ended up talking to some fair-

haired, slightly overweight, not a particularly attractive, dullard of a girl. She is telling me that I never speak to her at work. I say, 'I don't know you, why would I? You're welcome to come and talk to me though.'

The conversation continues in this rather arduous, dull way until she says something like 'it's all pointless'. I don't remember the context or if I was even listening to what she was saying at the time but there was something about this statement that hit me in the gut like explosive diarrhoea. It's not as if I've never heard this statement vocalised before, still, at this particular time in space it had a profound effect on me. Whilst she continued to jabber on, I stood up and quickly walked away in a slight swaying motion towards the men's toilet. I rushed into the cubicle to avoid the animals that were pissing in the metal trough that they may as well have been drinking from. I slammed the door shut and bolted myself in. I leant hard against the cold tiled wall of the toilet pushing against it whilst crying with a great intensity. Although I had suspected it for some time and perhaps I'd simply been ignoring it I knew then that I, and everything else around me, was completely insignificant and indeed "pointless". I found myself repeating 'Nothing means nothingness, nothing means nothingness' over and over like a restrained mental patient. I may have actually stolen this line from a film. I think it was 'I Love Huccabbees', a film I dearly love (not enough to remember this part clearly) and the only film I have ever watched three times in a row although I was rather depressed at the time and drinking quite heavily.

You have to be careful not to confuse films with real life. Sometimes you find that, because you have seen so many films that have covered almost every scenario and emotion that man has ever experienced, you don't know if your own actions are actually real or if you're acting them out as if you were being filmed and you're going for the Oscar. Everything imagined and realised in third person. I had this very same experience when I was in hospital after my father's triple heart bypass had gone badly wrong and subsequently nurses and machines were keeping him alive. The surgeon or consultant or whoever they were, casually told us (My mother, sister, uncle, brother-in-law and I) that they were going to turn the life support off. It was delivered with what felt like a real indifference as if they were telling you that your car failed its MOT. I know they do this every day and of course they can't get attached to their patients but it still seemed cold.

This was quite a shock to us as we had been previously informed that there was only a 5% risk of failure. We later found out they meant 50%. A bit of a major fucking clerical error I would say. We were told that his heart hadn't been strong enough to survive the operation and that, with each passing hour, each one of his organs was failing and being poisoned now that his liver and kidneys were no longer functioning properly, which I know would have pissed my dad off as he was a firm believer in donating his organs and even offered his body for scientific research.

After composing ourselves, we separately each took turns to walk down the lonely hallway of the hospital towards where my father lay. On arriving in the ward I see his chest rising and falling unnaturally, as he's being pumped with air and fluids through rubber tubes. His chest had been opened up and his insides were clearly visible with wires and pipes coming out of him like he had been impaled whilst trying to escape from Doctor Octopus. I'm alone in the room with my dad. The long white curtains are surrounding us and there's the constant sound of various beep, beep, beep noises made by the machines keeping him alive. I looked at him. This man, who now looked like a stranger to me although he had in many ways always been a stranger to me and I to him? How can you live with someone for 24 years and still have no idea who they were and still not really have anything to say to each other? I don't think we ever really had a heartfelt conversation. He certainly didn't know who I was but he seemed to love me, more so in my later years. I leant over and held my Dad quite awkwardly with plastic wires and tubes digging into my chest and head and I began to say my goodbyes. I remember little of what I said or perhaps I prefer to forget. What do you say to someone you have known for 29 years that you will never see again? Is there a sadder word than never? I know that I told him I loved him and I would miss him though in many ways, he was already dead despite the mechanical breathing. Here I am, alone with my dying father and I don't feel real even though I'm crying audibly and wildly and I felt as though I myself might die from hyperventilation, or that I at least wanted to die at that moment. I was in my own shit film. Am I being a real person? Was this a real experience? Was I really upset? Am I upset now? My eyes well up as I recall it. Another movie moment? Is this

tear real and is it for him or for me? Does anyone really give a fuck about anyone or when people die are they just crying for themselves because 'they' will miss them or 'they' will be alone or is it because people are so terrified of dying that we ball like a newly-born child in the hope that the rivers they fill with their tears will wrap them up and float them away to some warm, safe, sun-filled utopia where there's no such thing as fear and death is nothing more than a forgotten idea someone made up in a fairy tale just to scare children.
That's not quite true, I'm angry. I love my sister, my mother and my dear friends. That's real.
We all came together to gather around my dad's bed whilst the doctor turned off his life support. This was most surreal experience of my life and not one I hope to repeat though at least he was surrounded by the people that loved him the most. Few get such a honourable death. One thing I will say for my Dad is he could have had the money to go private and perhaps would still be with us today but he vehemently believed in the NHS as an institution, and so do I, it's important to have free health care when one needs it and not be left to die in a ditch because you don't have the money for an operation. Perhaps he paid the ultimate price for that belief but at least he died believing in something, and how many us can say that? When they flicked the switch I tensed, a feeling of this is really it. This is the last time I will see my dad. Unexpectedly, after the switch was turned off, the machine continued to beep and we were all confused. Is he still alive? Even without the life support? Has he pulled through? But no, as we stood there unsure as

to what had happened, they told us he had passed away and it's not his heartbeat making the beeping noise, it's the machine. It's not like in the movies where the machine goes beep, beep, beep, beep, beeeeeeeeep. I would have thought they could have at least told us that!!??
And so he was gone.
It is the strangest thing to watch someone so alive and animated and then, just like that, they are as cold and as still as a stone. The saddest memory I have of that day was when the nurse came in to the waiting room after and gave my mum her late husband's engagement and wedding rings. That more than anything seemed to make it real and my mum broke down at that point having been remarkably strong up until then. I too broke down in tears. It hurt me so much watching her like that, I've never seen my mum cry like that before, and the pain in my chest and stomach of my own teary convulsions tore a hole in me that I can still feel today. My older sister from memory was far more composed but perhaps she had her own demons to deal with. I respected my dad a great deal even if there were many things I did not like about him, more so when we were kids he was not always so kind to me & and even more so my sister. He was not afraid to die and we found out that although his whole body was completely fucked they were able to use the corneas from his eyes to help a stranger regain their sight. That's pretty fucking cool. Well done dad, maybe I will see you again some day, but neither of us really believe in any of that, do we.

x Ch-ch-ch-changes x

When there's grit in your eye and you are blind, you're being attacked, you feel vulnerable, confused, disoriented, upset and very, very, very angry, one tends to lash out.

x Monday, fun-day, happy days x

I adore Mondays as much as the next
man/woman. I've always wondered if the
derivative of woman was the word, *womb* plus
Man. A *womb-man*. The b is silent so it
sounds like woman as if said by a
Neanderthal, 'woommaann'. I am generally
quite miserable on a Monday as many are.
This is not an original thought. I find it
virtually impossible to be optimistic about
anything on this, the worst day of the week.
I suppose that this is not completely in my
control as I suspect the mixture of
chemicals that remain in my blood stream are
not helping. This issue of Monday dread
subsequently ruins my Sunday evenings.
I begin my day as usual. I wake up in my
flat. Ah yes, my flat. Here is a brief
description of my domain. It is a one
bedroom flat, in a new build 4-storey block
above a Tesco Express/Metro/Mini or whatever
the fuck they're called. It has wooden
(laminate) floors with an open plan living-
and-dining area and Kitchen. Most of the
furniture such as my coffee table, kitchen
table, A-frame shelves are made from old
wood and scaffolding planks. I have a real
thing for wood. It makes me feel calm,
relaxed and at peace. I have a few framed
screen prints on the wall I picked up from
Dalston Print Club. How cool am I (prick)? I
also have a few animal skulls mounted onto
my wall, a fate I'm certain they hadn't
envisioned for themselves. On the shelf sits
a framed mouse's head stuck to butterfly
wings with black horns attached. This was a
gift from a woman I worked with from whom
you would not expect to receive such a gift
from, especially as she made it herself. She

looks very prim and proper however she did reveal that she was a Scouse Goth when she was younger. Next to the dead animals there is an axe and an antique steel fisherman's hook. When people see these items upon my wall they often say 'what if you get angry?' In reply I say 'Well, you have a number of rather large sharp knives sitting in your kitchen drawer but when you get angry you don't go and retrieve one and plunge it into someone's gut every time you have a disagreement do you?' To which they say 'oh yeah'.

You might say my place looks like a Scandinavian wood cabin in a flat that looks too new. I have lived in 7 different places since I moved to London and have managed to sleep with one of my flat mates at every abode. Sometimes two flat mates at the same abode. It's foolish behaviour because as soon as you screw someone you live with everything eventually goes to shit. Especially if they like you and then you stop sleeping with them and then you bring new girls back to the house and shag them in the room above theirs. Not very nice! I don't really know what was I thinking but that seems to be a continuing trend in my life, not knowing what I was thinking. I have lived with a random array of people over the years and I've been in London around 5 or 6 years now. The first place I lived in was Shepherd's Bush where I shared a little terraced shit hole, 2-floor flat owned by an old Irish couple fleecing the tourists. There was only one poxy mouldy shower between the 8 of us. There were mushrooms growing around the outside base of the shower, which is fine if you get peckish mid-wash but I can't say that I ever was. The 7 people I lived with were all

Antipodeans. There was a nice Australian guy called Matt who had dreadlocks which always looks a bit ridiculous, as he is a white gentleman. There were a few inconsequential flat mates who are not noteworthy, a fat Kiwi who didn't like me because I didn't speak to her because she said I didn't want to fuck her. She accused me of not befriending people if I didn't fancy them. I suppose that is true sometimes. She was fat *and* boring. I mean some of the dumb fuckers I've held conversations with just because they're attractive is bordering on the ridiculous. I'm a terrible human being. It's not to say that I consider myself to be particularly attractive either. I think I'm about average looking, however I do have charisma and that goes a long way.

There was Kelly the Kiwi, who as soon as I met her I thought, 'Oh shit, this is going to be trouble'. This was when I first moved to London and I was still carrying my small town ignorance and idiocy and wasn't all that confident in my abilities to get into to women's pants. I'd done alright for myself back in Leicestershire but these London folks I imagined are a very different kettle of fish. Anyway, at the time I had a girlfriend that I loved very much and still do. We remained close friends after we broke up. I think being in London as a new boy on the scene put a strain on the relationship, and it crumbled soon after my arrival, which is shame as she lived here. On hearing the news of our break up Kelly made a hint that she liked me when we were writing a song together in the kitchen. Before long she was riding me on my bed. She was so attractive it hurt but we had absolutely nothing in common. I chased her around the flat most nights in the following weeks trying to get

laid and she seemed to be losing interest. I
just wanted to fuck her so badly. It was
like heroin. I had to have her. She had a
beautifully toned tanned body. Very dark,
long brown hair and the best real tits I had
ever seen in my life. She looked a little
bit Native American (not the proper name for
indigenous people from that area of land)
mixed with Japanese. She was my first
experience of squirting too. When she was
riding me she drenched my stomach with her
muff juice. Fuck, that was exciting and when
she gave me a blowjob she had me cumming in
a matter of seconds, which is extremely
rare. God, I fancied her. She moved out
eventually and ended up getting with some
Scottish boring banker wanker, tut!
The second place I lived in was on
Caledonian Road, the Holloway end. There I
only snogged a moody Swiss girl but I later
slept with the Hungarian girl after I left.
She had broken up with her boyfriend and
asked to meet up. We ended going back to
mine in a flat-share that I lived in in
Camden at the time and we were both pretty
damn pissed. We fucked on my bed in the dark
and when we were done she went to the
bathroom but she was so drunk she couldn't
find it and I found her wondering and
swaying around the landing drunk with blood
pouring out of her vagina. That'll never
come out of the carpet. It was cream as
well.

The third place I lived in was, as I just
mentioned, in Camden. It was a first and
second floor flat in a Victorian semi-
detached house that, as usual, was also
pretty run down. I lived with two girls and
one lad. The lad, Keith, was a decent geezer
but I could smell the stench of his room

when I passed it, even with the door closed. God knows how he convinced any woman to go in there with him. If his room smells like that, what the hell does his dick smell like? The two girls I lived with were a short dark-haired girl called Gemma who was a bit of a control freak, and a blond dizzy skinny girl called Kaz who was a paranoid depressive who I would have liked to have screwed but I think she was banging Keith, and we had not one single thing in common, and by the end both the girls hated me because I told Kaz to fuck off once over a cleaning argument. Luckily they both moved out and two new girls moved in. One was a fat but a loveable Ozzie girl I forget the name of and I affectionately named her Nigel. We screwed just the once as she was sleeping in my bed because we had a party and there was about 10 people sleeping over and I just sort of slipped it in. She'd been after me for ages but I'm really not a chubby chaser. To my surprise I came in less than a minute. I was not expecting that to happen. It's strange though. Often the girls you think you fancy the most can be the ones that take the longest for you to climax with. The other girl that moved in was a blonde, pretty, Jack Daniels-drinking, cigarette-smoking, leather jacket-wearing, rocker Norwegian called Solveig who had a strong but sweet smelling vagina. It was always soaking wet whenever we got down to it. I regret misunderstanding the situation with her. I thought we were just screwing for convenience but when I brought another girl back I found her crying in the kitchen. Sorry about that!

The fourth place I lived in was a brief 6 months in Forest Hill with my ex girlfriend

though I slept in a different room as we
were trying to be just friends. She was
doing me a favour because I had been made
redundant.

The 5th place I lived in was Kentish Town
with two of my band mates and I only fucked
one of them but that was whilst they were
sleeping and so that person still doesn't
know. If you're reading this Andy or Chris,
ask yourselves, did you ever wake up one
morning with a mildly aching but curiously
stimulated anus?

The 6th place I lived in was Bethnal Green.
I lived there for 3 years and I'd say this
was my favourite house share I'd lived in.
Sorry lads! I preferred the location and we
drank a lot. It felt like a place where
things were happening creatively. There is
an abundance of street art and tattoo shops
and old trendy pubs. We had a lovely group
of flat mates in our 3-floored, new-build
house. We had a piano in the living room,
which really made it feel homely, especially
when someone was playing it. We had quite a
large lounge / dining room and I used to
hold folk nights there every few months. I'd
invite musicians and singers to come and
play unplugged in our living room. We had
some really special evenings there. We even
had a weird French macabre style brass band
play one evening.
That was the last place that I lived in a
house share. It had its moments and we had
some damn fun drunken evenings, but there's
always boring politics about cleaning and
all that bullshit, and I fell out with a
couple of them and it didn't help that once
again I slept with one of them. Stupid boy!

Anyway back to the present. The alarm on my phone goes off. It is a very annoying alarm sound as my theory is that you're more likely to wake up if it's irritating. I used to have a classical clavier alarm sound and it never woke me up as, when I was still in that between sleep and consciousness like state, it made me feel like some sort of 16th century king laying in their oversized, goose feather filled bed and I just floated back to sleep.

I get in the shower. I get out of the shower. I dry myself with a dark grey towel and clean my teeth with a pink toothbrush. I can't watch other people clean their teeth it makes me cringe. Just thinking about it makes me shudder.

I put on my underpants, which are small and quite similar to superheroes' pants. At least that's how I see it. Some other people think they look ridiculous. 'Disgusting' is even a word I've heard used to describe them. I've often fantasised of being a super hero. Like many others that thought they were the only ones that favoured Wolverine, he too is my favourite. I suppose because he still seems mostly human and is not so sickeningly goody two shoes and all righteous like the others, and Superman can just do too much. The problem with being Wolverine is that, what happens if you get really angry whilst fingering a young lady and you accidentally shoot one of those razor sharp steel spikes up her cunt and give her an early period? I pull on my dark grey skinny jeans, a clean pair of socks (a great feeling) and pull on my leather boots. I put on a grey marl crew neck t-shirt as per normal and slip on my vintage blue denim jacket on, with my collar up. I like the arms to be a bit too short. I don't know why exactly, maybe it's my height issue again, but I do like it when my wrists protrude out of the cuffs. It's the same with a shirt. I feel like a kid if clothes are even slightly too big and someone might shout out 'is that your dad's?'

This is pretty much my staple get-up. It certainly saves time thinking about what I'm going to wear. One of the good things about being tattooed is that you're already accessorised so most of the work is done for you. I grab the book I'm reading and throw it in my khaki Fjallraven rucksack. I go to the kitchen, I'd love a cup of tea but as usual I don't have the time. I open a can of tuna fish and feed the eagerly awaiting Scout. Scout, as you may have guessed, is a mermaid. She is not a mermaid, which would be ace though. I think they might be extinct. No, it is in fact my dear pussycat, aged 2, female and has had her sexual organs removed. I am a bastard. She is part Bengal, part tabby. She was purchased from a pair of pikey chav scumbags. As a consequence Scout has a damaged tear duct in one eye and she cries excessively and so it results in lots brown goo spots (cat tears dry brown) left all over the house where she affectionately wipes her face on my possessions and white walls. I say my farewells, 'bye Scout' and she looks at me as if to say, 'I'm not sure what you're trying to say. I'm a cat!'

I leave through the dark green security gate of the block that is there to keep us middle class safe from the peasants that roam around West Green Road and outside of William Hill (a betting shop). Why are there always the most betting shops in the poorest areas? If that's not proof that betting doesn't pay off, I don't know what is. On this road alone there must be at least 10 of

them. The money-grabbing fuckers couldn't care less if these hopeless wasters fuck up their own - and potentially their families - lives. As long as there's plenty of gold in the coffers that's all these greedy twats care about. That reminds me, I should a put tenner on the 2 o'clock. I continue to make my way down this miserable road on which there doesn't, amongst the 60 or so shops, seem to be a single one I would consider of any use. Unless you want to place a bet, eat tortured chickens or buy a wig or phone card for Nigeria. Even the restaurants are a complete joke. They are decorated like someone's dodgy living room or not decorated at all, with paint peeling off the walls. It's a fifteen-minute walk to Seven Sisters tube station. I would get the bus but it takes the same amount of time as walking. Far too many people cram onto a bus that stops every 100 metres and is only going 5 minutes down the road. Lazy bastards. Some wait longer for a bus than the time it takes the bus or even themselves to make the journey on foot. Anyway I need the exercise following the weekend of self-abuse.
The train thunders into the station and there is always a temptation or at least a curiosity to just jump in front of it and end all of this bloody misery. Things can't be that bad and also a certain amount of cowardice prevent me from jumping to my death. In London, no one gives a toss if you kill yourself, they're all too busy being annoyed that you didn't do it at home because you've made them 10 minutes late for work. Plus it wouldn't be fair on my mother and sister, or is that just another cowardly excuse. The train comes to a halt and I can clearly see that there is no chance of me getting a seat, which is often the case at

this time of day. So we all cram into this
overheated, steel can on wheels and try our
best not look at each other, or acknowledge
that anyone else exists. We murmur under our
breath at the discomfort of being squashed
into this claustrophobic space that isn't
exactly cheap. I compose myself as the train
tries to close its doors 3 times due to some
fuck being stuck in the entrance. Eventually
the train gains momentum and we're slowly
dragged into the hot depths of the dark
tunnel, like when a killer whale bites down
onto a worn out seal's tail and slowly pulls
it off a floating sheet of ice into a dark,
glum, watery grave, whilst the seal looks
into camera with a resigned expression.
I'm now sitting on the Central Line having
made the transfer from the Victoria line. It
is a little quieter now and I get a glorious
seat and I can relax. At least that's what I
was hoping. When we get to Lancaster Gate,
some feckless moron gets on with his mate
and proceeds to start swinging around the
carriage like a retarded ape with ADD. He is
around 35, black, about 5,11, wearing army
shorts, a black worn t-shirt and a pair of
dirty army boots. It's quite clear he is
making everyone aboard visibly
uncomfortable. The dickhead approaches me
whilst I'm reading Time Out and although I
keep my eyes lowered the twat doesn't of
course have the social skills to notice I
have no desire to interact with him and he
taps on the corner of the magazine and says,
'Hey, nice art,' in a surprising Scottish
accent. I don't know why it's surprising
that he has a Scottish accent but then again
I think he may well be the only black
Scottish person I've ever met. I guess black
people don't love the cold, neither do I. He
then shows me some shitty black army tattoo

he proudly displays on his upper left arm. Fuck me, if these are the muppets fighting to protect the empire then the Queen had better start packing and heading to a hidden underground bunker right now because we're all fucked! The moron continues swinging around spreading his sour, pungent bodily odour around the carriage. I'm contemplating saying something but him and his mate are clearly deranged and given that they're in the army I'm not going to have much of a chance against them if they turn nasty. The atmosphere in the carriage is tense as the guy continues to draw attention to himself. Fortunately, the pair of twerps get off the train at Park Royal 10 minutes later and there's a sigh of relief from the remaining ordinary people on the train. Whatever ordinary means or at least ordinary enough to hide their thoughts of smashing those guys brains in and pulling their spines out through their mouths and being showered in their gushing blood whilst simultaneously being sucked off by two teenage schoolgirls in pop socks. I arrive at my destination, Hanger Lane. I get off the train and proceed to walk to our head office, which is based in the middle of an industrial estate because the people I work for are cheap, money-mongering, fuck heads. I hate them with a passion. They are a stinking pile of cunt. Stream Creek is the name of the company. My profession is footwear design, however it is design for the high street so it's somewhat watered down for middle England losers and chavs, and I'm sick to the back teeth of it and the fucking wankers I have to spend 9 hours a day with. I've never worked anywhere more miserable in my entire life. The whole of the staff of which there are around 1,000 all hate their jobs, the company, their manager, their fellow staff and subsequently themselves. Pretty much every girl/woman that works there is a chav. Even the older women are chavs. The head of design on women's wear looks like a leathery brown slapper on her way out to some small town nightclub in the early 90's called 'Slags!' There are a lot of women that wear hats at Stream Creek. And I don't mean beanies. I mean big stupid 'fashion' felt hats. Hats that are bigger than any original idea they have or will ever have conceived and they wear these hats INSIDE the fucking office whilst sitting there at their shit, cheap computer typing an email or filling in a spreadsheet. What's the wrong with these degenerates? These are the very people that have a full Instagram page with only photos of their own stupid face pulling some pouty idiotic face with their peace sign hand gesture or even worse… pictures of food! Who gives a FLYING FUCK WHAT YOU'RE HAVING FOR DINNER!!!. Everyone's eaten dinner before. Fucking billions of us. It's not a new phenomenon. It's just your fucking dinner. EAT IT!! That's what it's there for. To be eaten. How is it that some people can barely feed themselves and some people are advertising their meal! In America there's some guy who tries to eat more food than humanly possible. Only America could create such an ignorant and perverse TV show. It's called 'Man Versus Food'. It should be called 'Greedy Fat Cunt Versus Virtue'.

From my experience, girls that wear hats are usually the dullest people that you're likely to encounter and they're trying to fool you into thinking that they're cool and interesting by wearing them. What I have learnt is that hats are in fact a substitute for a personality. Avoid wearers of hats at all costs. Around 10 people must leave Stream Creek every week and 10 new unknowing victims join every Tuesday morning. The Stream Creek building is surrounded by a barbed-wire fence and if that isn't a sign to run for the hills, I don't know what is. It couldn't feel more like a prison. All they need now is an armed guard in a tower ready to sniper any hopeless employee who attempts to escape before 5.30pm. Alternatively you could just give all the staff one of those neck braces that explode when you leave the perimeter like in the film The Running Man. I enter the building and the dread instantly sets in. I have been here far, far too long. It's already been 4 years and I need to get out of here. I begrudgingly turn on my computer and go and make myself a cup of tea whilst it fires up. I fully appreciate that I should perhaps be more grateful to have this 'creative' job and I know others must think it quite glamorous, but fuck it, it really isn't unless you think sitting around a table listening to a load of fashion wank shafts make up words that aren't in the English dictionary because they don't have the ability to articulate the technicalities. The fashion industry must have one of highest concentrations of narcissistic morons that genuinely believe that what they do is actually important. Sure, it is better than working in a shop, or in an airport, or many of the other mundane jobs available, however I just can't bring myself to feel that way.

Whilst I'm waiting in the queue for my tea I notice a fat girl brandishing a can of Coke Zero whilst in the other hand gripping a king sized Mars Bar as though someone might try to wrestle it from her. Not these skinny bitches mate, you've no worries there. She says to her friend 'I'm sure these Mars bars are getting smaller.' The Mars bars have stayed exactly the same size love, it's just that you've got bigger. There appears to be something of a contradiction in her purchase. One doesn't cancel out the other. You may as well just drink the coke you really want and do some fucking exercise for once in your life so when you climb a flight of stairs or shag someone for more than 2 minutes you're not in danger of having a heart attack.

I return towards my desk with my cup of tea hoping to avoid any conversations with anyone on the way. I am not the person to talk to on a Monday... or Tuesday or Wednesday or Thursday come to think of it. On a Friday I might actually be what you might call 'pleasant'. Maybe I could even be considered to be charming and funny. That must be how I managed to fuck a small population of the females in this office, although still not as many as I would have liked. That's the problem with an office being situated in the middle of nowhere it makes it virtually impossible to get laid apart from at the Christmas party. The pub nearby looks like a Harvester so everyone sods off back to wherever they came from so one has to be opportunistic, and I unashamedly am. I don't see why anyone should feel guilty for wanting to fuck people. It's in our genes, we're still animals but we're controlled by cognitive, oppressive and societal views. All male mammals want to procreate with as many females as possible we simply can't help it. Staying with one woman is an unnatural phenomenon that only we Homo sapiens partake in because it hurts our feelings if our partner shags anyone else. Don't get me wrong, I too also believe in this. Loyalty counts for a lot and having the strength not to do that which your every instinct wants you to do shows a real inner strength and consideration for the person you love. That is why I am still single. Unless I know I am completely into a person, and know I can remain faithful to them, then I won't get involved. Well now it's for nothing less than love but perhaps I'm setting the bar of expectation too high.

Most of the boring retards I work with never have anything interesting to say to each other. You have a group of individuals that don't really know each other that well because they're so busy working, the only time that they get chance to converse is the 20 minutes they get for lunch and that conversation consists of on Mondays, 'what did you do at the weekend?' and by Wednesday it's 'what are you doing this weekend?'. It's mind numbing to say the least. I try my best to avoid being drawn into these monotonous chats however sometimes it's simply unavoidable and I find I'm boring myself and then I hate myself and the other person for making me so god damn boring. I sometimes whisper to them so quietly that it's barely audible, 'I hate you!'

As I begin to dredge through my many emails, my archenemy approaches me. Pete Pipps. He is a cunt. He is a big fat, bald, fuck pig that looks like a man-baby with a permanent red rash on his fat milky head. He looks like a thumb with a face. I think he must cut his hair with a knife and fork or a bit of granite. He looks like Darth Vader when he takes his helmet off. He doesn't appear to have a jaw line or even a chin. It is

almost impossible to tell where his head ends and his neck begins. He looks to be around 40 years of age but he is in fact 28, much to the amazement of every person who is later informed of this. I often like to type some sort of derogatory sentence about him on Microsoft Word but in a font so small he can't read it so that if he is standing behind my desk I can sit there wantonly slagging him off. As the fat fucker heads towards me the depression sets in. He has the nerve to say, 'Mornin' mate!'
I am not and never will be *your* mate, mate! He only ever seems to wear Ted Baker clothing as I think they are the only shirts that fit the fat cunt. His greeting is conveyed in his broad Bradford accent. He couldn't be more of a northern stereotype if he tried. He is the most uncultured man I have ever met. He is basically a fat Carl Pilkington but less charming and charismatic and much ruder. He asks me to do some new patterns on a loafer that is selling well and I reluctantly agree. I hate him. Even worse, tomorrow I have to fly to India with this planet-sized bastard. The plane will probably plummet into a mountain carrying that massive twat. Did I mention I hate him?

x Fears x

I essentially only have 3 real fears.

1. Heights. I'm not a big fan of heights. It may be perhaps because I fell off a railway bridge onto a concrete road and smashed my head when I was 14 and ended up in a coma but I think I've always been a bit of a fucking wimp when it came to heights. It's a shame because I like hiking.
2. Bread & other food going mouldy. But mostly bread.
3. Running out of booze.

x Clean up that mess x

5.30am, my phone rings, it's the taxi driver that's taking me to Heathrow airport. From his accent I deduct that he is of an eastern European origin. I pull my silvery grey, hard-shelled suitcase (never had a suit in it) across to the other side of the road around 10 minutes later, after I've finished me cup of tea. It will be some time till I enjoy a good cuppa. The driver takes my bag and puts it in the boot of his Toyota Yaris. Toyotas must be cheap. Nearly all of these eastern European taxi drivers seem to own one. As usual the guy doesn't have a Scooby Doo where he is going and he relies on his phone's satnav, which means hitting all the major traffic jams. The guy has awful bodily odour and stabs on his accelerator constantly which makes it virtually impossible to relax and get the shut-eye I was aching for. At least the guy doesn't attempt any conversation, which I am grateful for. We get to Heathrow an hour or so later and I head into the airport. I self check in because BA don't want to pay anyone to do it anymore, just like Tesco or the other tight-wad supermarkets where you have to do everything yourself even if it takes 3 times longer, resulting in mounting queues of disgruntled people asking themselves 'why can't this idiot operate this simple piece of machinery?' which is exactly what I think every time and then it happens to me although I'm sure it's not *my* fault this time.
I reluctantly meet fat head Pete Pipps in Jamie's Italian for breakfast and we make polite conversation, pretending that we

don't despise each other. We always check in separately and get an aisle seat so we don't have to sit next to each other. I watch a few films drink a few gin and tonics until I'm tired enough to hit the hay. Fortunately we are in business class, which makes sleeping a possibility but we're still surrounded by overweight middle-aged men that fart throughout the entire journey, making you gag and making the air even more stale than it already is. You always get these businessmen-type losers on a flight that stand at the bar of the plane and try to chat up the poor hostess who's seen better days and has to laugh at their awful 90's jokes that weren't funny even then. Twats! ('Twats' was the name my ex-girlfriend told me my first business should be called).

We exit the plane 9 hours later and a wall of humidity hits us like someone opening the door to a volcano and we're all instantly baked and perspiring profusely, especially the fat middle-aged fellas and, of course, Pete's back is soaked and he's visibly uncomfortable which makes me smile from ear to ear, given that I am merely mildly warmer than I should like. I put my sunglasses on and cross the concrete like I've just arrived at the beginning of a rock tour. My fans mustn't have got the info that I was coming as none of them are here to cheer my arrival? If only, if only, Jesus!

A few days into the trip and we've already driven about 500 miles, visited 4 factories in the depths of Indian hell and flew 3 additional times and my patience is beginning to wear thin. Fortunately tonight we are staying in Mumbai at a 5 star hotel (5 star for India) and we're being joined for dinner by the shirts team from Stream

Creek. This comprises of the owner's son
Will, who has ADHD, my design manager Mark
and two other women, a buyer and a designer.
When you see familiar people in an
unfamiliar environment you fall in love with
them and cling to them for dear life even if
in the UK you couldn't give a flying fuck
about them. It's like a real English cup of
tea or a bacon sandwich. I mean having a
bacon and egg sandwich after not having had
one after a week is divine, but women!!...
Actual real English women!!!! Fuck a duck!
It's like you've found the lost city of
Atlantis. It's clear that the two women,
Lucy and Sarah, also detest the big fat
baby, though he of course doesn't notice
this and continues on with his dad-like
humour. Lucy is around 27 and Sarah is 31.
Lucy is the designer and Sarah the buyer.
Both are averagely attractive but in this
scenario they are goddesses. As we eat and,
in the excitement of keeping company with
fellow English-speaking compatriots,
everyone begins to get steadily drunk - but
not me and fatso. Fatso doesn't really
drink, also a sign of a twat. After we eat,
we go up to the hotel bar for a nightcap.
The giant baby as usual goes up to his
bedroom early, in the excitement he may have
some work emails to wank over and the
owner's son, Will, follows soon after. We
can at last have a bit of a laugh and have a
normal conversation with the absence of ADHD
boy and the humungous slab of meat man. I
inform them that I am going for a piss and a
cigarette knowing they have all recently
been themselves.

I return a little out of breath and a little
bit wet. 'Raining outside was it?' Mark, my
manager, says.

'Yeah, a flash flood!' I say smiling and the girls laugh a little. Now there's just me, the two girls and Mark who I actually quite like but I really want him to piss off right now and unusually for him he does get an early night, well 1am anyway. It must be the jetlag. The bar is dead by this point and the waiter is eyeing us up to leave. I say, 'Shall we go to my room, there's plenty of booze in the mini bar?'

'Yeah why not.' Lucy says.

We go into my room, which is fairly modern with a beige carpet and marbled bathroom floor. We continue to drink wine and whatever else we can find the mini bar, which is profusely expensive and we chat about random crap. We're starting to get quite pissed now. We start to playfully push each other around a bit and before I know it we're having a full on wrestling match for domination of the bed. It's me against the two of them and we're fighting for ownership of the bed like pirates on a small one-man island surrounded by sharks. I win of course which bodes well in such a situation as it states your dominance as long as you don't go to far and end punching one of them in the face. What girl wants to fuck a pussy when they already have one? When we get our breaths back and I have proved my masculinity I agree to let them share my bed space and we start getting pretty close to each other. In noticing this and in a playful manner, Lucy says 'get your dick out then!' which takes me back slightly as I hadn't envisioned such forwardness but I consider this for a second to see if she's winding me up or not and by the look in her eye and her hands pulling at my belt I assume she isn't. She undoes my belt, I unzip my flies and I pull my dick out as requested and Lucy takes hold of it and begins to wank me off in a drunken manner. By this time we're snogging fully and wildly. Our tongues lashing around like the Kraken. She pulls off her trousers and knickers at which point I turn around and start to kiss Sarah. Whilst kissing Sarah I take my right hand middle finger and insert it into Lucy's very wet hole. Lucy by this point is completely naked. Sarah is a little more reluctant to remove her clothes but I manage to get her to pull her skirt up and I pull her kickers aside and slide the middle finger of my left hand into *her* pussy. I'm now fingering the two of them and taking turns to kiss them whilst Lucy is still giving me a hand job. Lucy is gagging for more and gets onto her back, spreads her legs and tells me to fuck her. I politely oblige her and push my cock inside her. I'm not particularly delicate as it's already 4am and I'm filthy drunk. I'm fucking Lucy pretty deep and I'm getting into it but I see Sarah is tired and waning a little at the lack of attention and is face down so I slip my finger into her again and she livens up a bit. Lucy is really getting into it now and decides she wants me to fuck her from behind in bathroom. She leads me behind her into the bathroom, puts her hands onto the hard cold marble sink top and tells me to fuck her. I take my hands either side of her hips and push the full length of my cock inside her. She is absolutely soaking wet. We are really going for it and I can see our reflection the mirror which gets me even more excited and she's telling me to fuck her even harder which excites me even more. It's always nice to know they're enjoying it. Lucy cums easily about 3 times in a row and ends up showering me with pure

unadulterated vaginal juice. I've only ever fucked 3 squirters in my life and I've fully enjoyed the experience every time. It makes a bloody mess but it's pretty damned ace and hey, this ain't my bathroom! After Lucy's finished giving me a good soaking, she says she's done. I on the other hand after fucking her for about 20 minutes, being drunk and wearing a condom cannot cum and the bitch won't let me finish her off without one. She strolls back into the bedroom, collapses on the bed and falls asleep in a second, leaving me with a useless erection. I see Sarah is stirring a little and I lay on top her and start to kiss her neck. She is still laying face down but her arse is peeking out from under her skirt. She doesn't want me to put my cock in her after Lucy but I tell I used a condom. I remove the condom and slide myself inside her. She doesn't seem 100% sure but once it's inside her she seems happy enough. I get into a slow steady motion and this being one of my favourite sexual positions I can feel the blood and excitement rising. I fuck her for a couple of minutes more until I pick up a bit of pace and blow the whole of my load inside her. Now I am content, I can sleep at last. Maybe India isn't so bad after all! 87, 88.
Beep!, beep!, beep!, beep!, beeeeep!........bep!, bep!, beep!, beep!.... my alarm is going off 30 minutes after I put my head down!!! Fuck it's 8am already and my head is complete mush. The girls are fast asleep, as they don't have to go to work today as the lucky lasses are flying home later on. It's an awful feeling when you're stuck in the dark depths of India and people leave to go home to Blighty before you. It's like being left on a sinking ship and the

people on the life raft are promising
they'll come back for you. I am still
completely pissed out of my brain hole. I
stumble across the room and into the
bathroom, looking at the sink and
remembering the wondrous fucking that
occurred there. I get in the shower hoping
it will revive me like the sun revives Clark
Kent. Of course, I'm so fucked it doesn't
help one iota. I throw some clothes on and
head down to the lobby where Will and Mark
are waiting. My brain feels like someone
took it out of my head, slammed it in the
door a few times, put it back in upside
down, and poured petrol on it. When you're
still that drunk you try your level best to
pretend that you're sober and you act
unnaturally normal although I must reek of
booze. My teeth still feel furry despite
having only just cleaned them. 'Morning.' I
say. 'Morning.' they reply in stereo.
'Have you seen Pete?' Will asks.
'No.' I reply.
'I'll call his room.' Will goes up to
reception to call Pete's room, as Pete is
not answering his mobile.
'He's not answering. That's odd. He must be
still asleep? That's not like him at all.'
Pete is militant when it comes to being up
on time which means everyone else has to be
too when he's around. Prick!
'I'll go and knock on his door, sir.' says
the hotel receptionist. This takes some time
and Will is becoming agitated and restless,
as he has no patience whatsoever. I am more
relaxed as I know something they don't. 20
minutes later the receptionist returns
looking like he's seen a ghost and is quite
out of breath. 'Please sirs, one moment.'
5 minutes later the hotel manager comes out.
He is a smartly dressed man proud of his

position and achievements having started as a bellboy originally from the slums some 40 years previous.

'Please can you follow me into my office gentleman.' The manager says.

We, or at least Will and Mark look at each other not understanding what is going on but we agree to follow him.

'Please… sit down!' Says the manager, gesturing towards the chairs.

'There appears to have been a terrible accident.' The manager says.

'Where's Pete?' Will says interrupting him.

'I'm afraid to have to tell you that your colleague has had a fatal accident. Your colleague has had a fall in the shower and in the event, he hit his head and this morning when my colleague entered his room he found your colleague to be deceased. I'm certain he would have felt no pain as it would have happened very quickly.' The manager reveals to us.

Mark and Will are gobsmacked and look as if they have lost all power of speech. I think Will's probably most concerned, not because he cares but because a member of his staff has died on a work trip, and I'm sitting there trying my very best not to let a smile slip and look in shock, when of course I'm not in shock as I have known what happened, from the moment it happened, because I was there.

When we checked in, I managed to pilfer the second copy of his room key card when he was fishing out his passport and the receptionist had their back turned. You often get two copies however you wouldn't notice if they only gave you one as it doesn't always happen.

After we finished dinner last night and Pete went to bed, this is the point that I excused myself and went for a 'cigarette and a piss' knowing that roughly in my head it would give me enough time to carry out the following. When Pete goes to bed, one thing I know for sure is that he'll get in the shower first. I go to his room at the end of corridor and put my ear to the door. I can hear the twat shuffling around as he comes close to the door, so close that I think he's going to open it. I hold my ground and he moves away again. I allow myself a controlled and quiet exhalation. I hear the sound of the shower coming on. I give it another minute or two in case he's waiting for the water to heat up or in case he's taking a shit. I very gently slip the key card into the slot and wait for the green light, which doesn't come on. Fuck!! Patience, patience. I slip it in again and... bingo!! It clicks green and I open the door slowly and carefully. I can hear Pete in the shower and he's singing some shit R&B song. Twat! The fat white blob secretly wishes he was slimmer, had hair, and was black. He couldn't be further from this reality if he was himself, and he is himself. I remove my t-shirt and lay it on his bed. I move towards the bathroom, one of those with no door. He's scrubbing away under his armpits facing away from me. I take position behind him. I bend both my legs so that my head is around the equal height of his spotty backside. I pull back my right arm and take my aim. As fast and as hard and as straight as I can, I launch my fist into the back of his left knee. I learnt this trick in the school dinner queue. My mate used to come up behind me and smash his fist into the back of my leg and embarrassingly you go down uncontrollably like a sack of spuds in front of the girl

you most fancy. As predicted, though with a
little uncertainty given the size of the guy
his leg crumples below him. Almost in slow
motion as he's descending he half turns his
thumb-shaped head towards me and by this
point I'm already up on my feet as his eye
catches mine. In a hundredth of a second I
can see the dread and realisation in his
terrified eyes of what's happening, which is
one of the most enjoyable moments of my
life. I return his look with a sadistic grin
in the knowledge of what's to come. This is
where time speeds back up as I take my
already returned right hand whilst we
exchanged glances and use it smash his
fleshy orb into the shiny, hard, steel
controls and... whollop!! I feel the full
force and the dead stop as his head engages
with the stainless steel mechanism and a
small spurt of blood shoots out, fortunately
away from me and up against the tiles in the
corner. Fuck, that was exhilarating!! I'm
breathing heavily with all the adrenaline
speeding around my veins at a thousand miles
a second. I watch his limp flabby body slide
down into the corner, making that long,
loud, rubbery squeaking noise that skin
makes against wet smooth surfaces and then
there's a soft thud as he lands. When he
comes to a halt his head is sideways on and
his face looks twisted and distorted as
though his last expression has been framed
in the horror he saw before his final
demise. The shower continues regardless,
pelting his face and diluting the remains of
the blood down into the plughole. I look
down on him and smile and I spit on his
stupid twisted dead face. I've never killed
before. Well I mean, I've killed before but
they were animals, literally. I killed a
rabbit whilst out ferreting with my idiot

mate in the countryside. I hit it on the back of the neck with a sort of karate chop it took a few goes though. I also shot a robin, right in the chest with an air rifle after another moronic friend of mine left bread out on his front lawn for the birds. This must be an international crime, one where Santa Claus sends a miniature helper to assassinate you in your bed by stuffing candy cane down your throat causing you to choke to death. May I, at this point, say that I deeply regretted both of these acts and in my defence I was only 14 and 12 years of age. I was easily influenced back then. I decided quite soon after that, that I despised those that kill animals for fun especially those pompous fox hunting, incestuous pricks.

I walk out of the bathroom, put my t-shirt back on, return his second key card to the dresser and open the door very slightly to check there's no one around and then swiftly exit and close the door quickly and quietly behind me. I walk calmly down the hall way singing 'Beyond The Sea' as I go. This all took a matter of minutes though it felt like an hour and in no time I was back with the others.

When we returned to the office in London, the news of course got there before we did. You could see people were struggling to know what to say to us. Most people never do know what to say when someone dies but he was not a popular person and although it's quite a shock to them at this point in time, I'm fairly certain that when the realisation that they don't have to work with the fat cunt anymore sets in, they'll be pleasantly relieved at his absence. Life continues as before.

x Back in the USSR x

It's raining. Welcome to England, not the USSR. I rather like the rain, as perpetual sunshine for some reason often depresses me slightly. I think it's because the sunshine represents people getting together in their cosy friendship groups sitting in parks having a BBQ, so when you find yourself alone and have no friends available it feels quite lonely. I do have friends although I'm sure it won't surprise you I don't have many. You must be thinking that I am quite the misanthrope, which is true and it's not. Mostly I just want the sun to sod off so I can stay in my flat and not feel guilty about shooting aliens in the face for a few hours. It is so addictive playing PS3 games. I have many fond memories of playing computer games on cold wintery days, all warm drinking tea inside. I can take drugs, drink booze, play a gig, but none of them take me to such a meditative state that computer games do. It's the only time I can truly forget about everything else in my life. I cherish it though that's the very reason I rarely play them because it stops me from doing anything else until the game is completed. These days it's a once-a-year Christmas treat to myself, if I've been a good boy.

It's 11am on Sunday and I'm sitting in my Danish rocking chair drinking a cup of tea out of my orange and cream Scandinavian looking mug with feathers on it, and in the background 'After You've Gone' sung by Al Jonson is playing out of my mac. I look up and see that my teak framed print of a Fox comprised of small black and white pin-up girls that is hung on my wall is at a slant once more. I'm sure my friends keep tilting it when I'm not looking or perhaps it's my cat. Ungrateful fur ball! Though she is one of the few things I have any great affection for. Earlier I pointed out a daddy longlegs (or crane fly) to her thinking that it might entertain her for a short while. This is the first time I have observed her understanding me pointing at something. It must be pretty exciting to have another living thing flying around seeing as she is imprisoned within my flat. I watch her follow the daddy-long-legs around the room, although at this stage it is well out of her reach. I wave my vest at the insect to get it to come a little lower, as this activity is going nowhere. As it comes into her range, Scout swipes at the daddy-long-legs. She catches it with her claw however the insect escapes, though I can see that it has sustained an injury and beginning to flail. With waning strength, it slowly descends to a more favourable height and Scout goes in for the kill. I admittedly and foolishly hadn't really considered the outcome and that death would be the result. I was just trying to entertain my cat for 5 minutes of its monotonous life. One forgets that these cute, furry creatures are stone cold killers. After she made the final crushing kill, and this part I didn't expect, she put it in her gob and swallowed it whole. The poor daddy-long-legs. Now doomed to the depths of Scout's intestines until it's shit out into her litter tray. It made me feel a bit sick. Scout just looked at me like nothing had happened and trotted off. Another life crushed and I'm an accomplice. It's a stupid thought really, given that I'm about to make my way back to

the Rose Café for a plate of pig death and
maybe, almost certainly, a cup of tea. No,
definitely. There's no question whatsoever.
I don't know why I said that. I've never in
my life been for pig breakfast and not had a
cup of tea. I deeply regret saying that,
maybe even more so than my assistance to the
death of that insect.

x Vote now x

'Do you want another cup of tea?'
It's Saturday a week later and I met Izzie
last night at a gig we played at the 333
Club in Shoreditch. She knows Andy the bass
player and let me know via him that she was
interested in me. When I first saw her I
thought to myself 'Wow, she is incredibly
attractive'. I certainly wouldn't have had
the balls to approach her and was surprised
at her candidness. Women very rarely make a
move on me after I've been performing on
stage. I'm not trying to sound arrogant but
I have a half decent voice and the band are
great and I have been told that women
sometimes do find us attractive however they
never pluck up the guts to talk to us, and
if I can't tell for sure if a stranger likes
me I very rarely have the stomach to speak
to them either. Pathetic! I'm fine talking
to women, just not complete strangers that I
have no reason to speak to. No, that's not
quite true, I am actually fine with that if
it happens organically. I find that when
you're at some bar or pub it's just too
blatant that you're only talking to someone
for one reason and when you watch other
dickheads at bars doing the very same thing
it's makes you feel ashamed of our male
species. It seems so charmless and tacky and
so the very last thing I want to do is look
like those boozed up, drooling sex pests.
The lads and I have been in a band together
for about 2 years or so now. We named
ourselves The Winter Kicks. Shit name right.
I think it's mostly my fault. No, it's all
my fault. We were attempting to come up with
a band name in the Captain Kidd pub in

Tobacco Dock whilst drinking very reasonably priced bitter. Sam Smith, I believe, is the brewery. I don't see why a pint of beer should cost you the earth after you've slogged your guts out at work all week. Sam Smith pints are much closer to what a pint should be but, Jesus, it's still an expensive hobby. It's the pricks that charge you £5 for a bottle of beer at some wank bar that vexes me.

We have recently entered ourselves into one of these band-conning competitions known as Battle Of The Bands, which is a foolish concept. No bands should be battling. That's not what music should be about. Nonetheless we are still rather green and hungry for a slice of success, and novice bands get very desperate, and so we entered ourselves even though it cost £50 to do so. The only thing I have ever achieved musically so far is tinnitus in my right ear. The way that you get through these dubious rounds is by bringing more people to the gig than the other bands and subsequently your friends vote for you by putting their hand up when asked. What an arsehole of a system. On that basis, if a bunch talentless punks show up with a bigger crowd than if the actual Beatles (in this scenario them being unknown), the shit band would go through and the Beatles would not.

We played our first round at The Bull & Gate in Kentish Town and we brought approximately 4 people. We must have had 1 more friend than some of the other douche bag bands because somehow we got through.

'That'd be lovely' I reply to Izzie.
She is very beautiful and I'm still in mild shock. I'm also surprised that she slept with me on a first date, and perhaps a

little disappointed. I'm a complete hypocrite when it comes to sleeping with someone on a first date. I pretty much always want to do it but if I like them I prefer it if they don't. If I don't care about seeing them again then it's brilliant. Perhaps if I meet someone and I get the feeling that this person could be 'it' maybe I'll be a bit more restrained. The problem is, I'll like them so much and feel like I'm in love and want to have sex with them. I always end up sleeping with many of my female friends. I can't help it. If you like someone it makes you attracted to them, and then you want to get closer to them but also sometimes you just like fucking each other. If I liked men's anuses I'd probably fuck my male friends (with their permission) too. I've considered homosexuality, however men's bum holes make me feel nauseous and my own bum hole is very small and it simply couldn't accommodate a big fat cock. Disappointingly we were both reasonably drunk and so I don't remember a great amount of detail though I know I enjoyed it. I think I'll see her again. That's probably a certain amount of arrogance on my part. I usually assume that they (the women) do want to see me again and in fairness they usually do but don't get me wrong, I've also been dumped my fair share of times too. 89.

x Expenses x

Its 5.30am Wednesday morning and I'm off travelling again on behalf of my beloved company Stream Wank Creek. We are travelling to Amsterdam from Stansted airport to do a spot of research, which means going around the competitions stores buying clothes and shoes to copy and steal their ideas. That's all my company does. They pretend that they are a brand even though all they do is simply rip off other brands at a more affordable price and make them trashier. They love to stick gold on just about every single garment or shoe on the women's wear. It's disgusting!
I am travelling with Alex and Dave. This means it should be a decent trip. They're both around my age and both are a decent laugh. Dave has long blonde hair and wears clothes that are too big for him and as a result he looks a bit like Kurt Cobain with a large head if you squint your eyes. Alex has a sizeable Shoreditch beard and has skinny black jeans and a pair of Doc Marten's shoes on, and they both sound a bit geezer-ish when they talk because they're southerners. I think they're from somewhere like Kent or Essex.
It's pretty cold as it's March, but there's clear blue skies and sunshine. We have a pleasant day walking around the shops and stopping for a hearty burger for lunch at some trendy joint where they refuse to serve food on plates.
After a leisurely day wondering the beautiful back streets of Amsterdam we drop off our bought samples back at the hotel. I also bought myself a nice thick navy melton nautical, Scandinavian style jacket and a

pair of Red Wing boots with chestnut
coloured leather uppers and full leather
soles. I say I bought them myself. In fact
my employer unknowingly paid for them. Seven
hundred and fifty quid's worth! Thanks
Stream Creek. We have a beer in the lobby
and head out for dinner. As the company are
paying we head to an expensive steak house
and order the best steaks and red wine
available. The restaurant has a dark red
interior and has a long dark red curtain
covering the inside of the front entrance to
keep the draft out. It's quite charming and
decadent. We get fairly merry swilling down
red wine and a few Peronis on top. We mostly
slag off Stream Creek and its employees and
little is said about Pete's death, now
having passed a few weeks ago. Fuck him! We
stay in there for a few hours and we then
eventually decide to leave the warmth of the
restaurant and into the cold crisp night air
of Amsterdam. The wind chill instantly hits
us in the face as soon as we step outside.
It's 12.30am. I pull my leather jacket
collar up and wrap it around my neck.
'Right. Who's up for a bit of window
shopping in the interesting part of town?'
Dave suggests.
Alex and I pull that face when you sort of
raise your bottom lip and chin in a
thoughtful, agreeable manner.
'Why not,' I reply.
We trundle off into the night and it's
fairly quiet other than a few drunken
tourists and the odd hot local, arty type
girl on their bike we all wish we could
follow home. They're the ones that look like
they're just too interesting to talk to you
or acknowledge your existence. After walking
for around 15 minutes crossing the bridges
over the canals, we arrive in the red light

district and there is a clear juxtaposition between the trendy, cool affluent part of the town and the seedy sex for sale section. It is noticeably not as well maintained. One of the first sex workers I see is a transgender male in a dimly lit window and he/she looks to be neither attractive as a man or a woman and it makes me feel a bit sick and creepy and a slight shiver shakes me inside of my jacket. There is a certain sheepishness about us as we peruse what's on offer. No one is saying much or perhaps they're just so engrossed in the view. I've no idea if they've ever fucked a prostitute and I don't let on that I have. Only once in China but I hadn't been expecting it. I was about 24 and I decided to get a massage in the hotel in Shenzen. After half an hour of very relaxing oily hand work the masseuse asked me 'you waaan penis massage?' after intentionally massaging my thighs near my cock and giving me an erection. There's only really one answer to that question. 'Yes!' I reply.

She gets a hand full of oil, peels back the sheet that's covering my cock and starts to work her hand up and down my shaft. The weird thing is she is wearing a kind of sports shell-suit so it's feels like you're getting wanked off at a leisure centre. It's pretty fucking brilliant though. Experience pays I suppose. The next evening I go back again and the same thing happens again but this time half way through she asks, 'you waaan sex?'

'Err, how much?' I don't remember the cost but it was a reasonable price after a bit of bartering.

We walk around for a bit and I see this one girl with amazing legs, the most resplendent

pair of tits and wearing black thick square-rimmed glasses and long jet black hair and a very tight black dress. Just looking at her made my cock twitch inside my skinny jeans. At this point I'm not quite sure what the game is, and if anyone's actually going to do this, so I reluctantly walk past her.
We pass a few average girls and then I see a busty, curvaceous, blonde Russian girl in the window and she's looking straight at me and, like every other prick that walks past, I think, 'she likes me!' I'm still a bit drunk at this stage so my inhibitions are reduced and I go over to her window, I ask how much and before I know it she is leading me downstairs to a tiny little basement room with a single bed, a mirror, a basket of condoms and some lube. On my descent I realise how cold I was out there and that my dick has shrivelled to a virtual vagina. I mention this to the prostitute and she says in her thick Russian accent 'Don't worry about it, I'll sort that out,' sounding quite militant. I'm laying flat on the bed naked and she put's a condom on my flaccid dick and pops it in her mouth. Even with a condom on I can feel the warmth and dampness of the inside of her mouth and true to her word, in a matter of seconds I'm standing to attention. After she sucks me for a bit she's asks 'Do you want to fuck me?'
Again there is really only one answer to such a question.
She climbs on top of me takes my cock in her hand and puts it inside her. It feels divine. She bounces up and down for a bit and grinds too but I'm thinking I want to be the one doing the fucking. I put her on her back, lift her legs high and wide apart. She's has a really beautiful pussy to say it's been getting smashed 10 times a night,

5 nights a week. Because she's a prostitute
you can just fuck them however you please
without feeling guilty about whether they
are enjoying it. You can do it just like how
they do it in porn. You can't really do that
with the general public. This is after all a
fantasy fuck. You get these pricks that pay
for a prostitute and spend their time trying
to make the prostitute cum. Fucking idiots.
I plunge in and out of her, deep and hard,
finding it difficult to decide whether to
stare at her tits or my cock going in and
out of her pussy. Anyway, it's not the worst
problem one can have. I know that we're on a
timer and I've got to make sure I blow my
load in her before my 20 minutes are up. I
decide to go for the true prostitute fucking
position and turn her over and get her on
her hands and knees. Her pussy is perfectly
formed and her arse a bronzed peach. I take
my cock and slide it back inside her and she
pushes back onto it. I take hold of her ass
cheeks and give her good hard ramming and I
know this is the ticket. Soon enough I am
cumming into my rubber cock jacket and I'm
done. I take a second to catch my breath and
enjoy it. She pulls away from my cock and
gets up like nothing's just happened. She
gives her fanny a quick wipe and she's ready
for the next customer. I give her the 100
euros that I later put on my expenses under
taxis. Thanks again Stream Creek. Perhaps
you do have some uses. 90.
Fully dressed I head back out into the cold
and I see Alex and Dave just stood there
freezing their tits off.
'What're you doing? Didn't you get one?' I
say.
'Er, nah, I didn't really fancy it' Dave
says. 'It's too cold and my dick's
shrivelled up.'

What a pair of pansies. All talk.
'Well thanks for waiting for me in the freezing cold whilst I was nuts deep in a warm vagina.' And I meant it. I had no idea where the hotel was.
'You're welcome!' says Alex, none too impressed.
On the flight home we are all seated separately and I find myself sitting in the aisle next to two French girls. They also have a male companion sitting in the seats behind us. They are chatting away and seem like a nice enough group of people, at least for French people anyway. Midway into the flight, they offer me some of their wine.
'Would you like some wine?' The girl furthest away asks me.
'That'd be nice. Thanks' I reply.
We make some small talk about where they've been and they ask me the same. When asked I tell them that I'm a shoe designer and as often is the case, more so with women than men, they are quite impressed which often takes me by surprise because it doesn't seem all that impressive to me. You should see some of the monstrosities I have designed on behalf of Stream Creek. The girl farthest away is blonde and chubby and not up to much. The one closest to me has shabby tied up long dark brown hair giving her a look of self-confidence though not taking her self too seriously. She's wearing a loose-fitting wide neck dark red jumper, a pair of vintage blue jeans and pair of tan brogues, and she sort of pouts every now then when she talks. It's not in a Posh Spice pouting way. It's more like a face one pulls when one's thinking. It's cute. It transpires that this group of frenchies live just around the corner from me so I say 'I have a taxi booked if you want to share it with me. It's

free because it's paid for by Stream Creek. It'll save you slogging it on public transport' They pull that face people pull when you tell them something they weren't expecting and feel a bit confused and not sure if it's rude to accept a free taxi. When the idea has sunk into their brains the girl closest to me, Camille, says, 'Ah, oui.' When we land it's pretty late, around 10.30pm. The cab I've booked turns out to be a big fuck-off people carrier with seats facing each other in the back, which I feel heightens my status with them a bit. A free ride and in luxury! Camille sits next to me and quite soon she has her head on my shoulder. When we're half way home I ask if anyone wants to come to my flat for a drink as all the pubs are closed as it's past 11pm. It's a fucking joke, really. London is one of the most highly visited tourist destinations in the world. It has a mass of multiculturalism, hundreds if not thousands of art galleries, live music venues, restaurants, museums and shit loads of pubs and they all pretty much close at 11pm. It's quite a joke and it's kind of embarrassing when people from other countries come to visit. Having said that, the underground is still not 24hrs and black cabs are not cheap. The only other option after 11pm is some sort of club and that really is not my scene. Even when I was 18 something didn't sit right with me about clubs but that's what everyone did at that age so you just went along with it and I assumed there was something wrong with me. Now I'm older I can comfortably say I hate nightclubs, they're shit. The lighting is shit. Bouncers are idiot shits. The drinks are expensive so that's shit. The toilets are shit with shit in them and shittest of all is that the music is really fucking shit! I hate fucking dance music. I still call it dance music because I never bothered to learn the technical differences between the various types of dance music such as minimal dub wank, or garage or drum and bass or electro speed cunt. So to me it's all dance music. When you go to somewhere like Berlin, they don't even leave the house until about midnight when they're going out to play. On the subject of Berlin I travelled there last year in the winter to go to Bread & Butter, which is a sort of branded fashion trade fair that's held in a massive ex-Hitler plane hanger. On the first day I travelled with an assistant buyer called Joe. Nice enough lad and pretty laid back. It was March and it was freezing cold in Berlin. After flying all the way to Germany we didn't even get into the show because I'm a designer and they only let buyers into the show because designers only go there to steal ideas. To gain entry, someone back at the office made me a fake business card that said 'Footwear Buyer' on it. The only problem was that the feckless retard that made it printed it out onto a standard piece of white flimsy paper so the card which you couldn't even call a card just flopped in your hand. The clues in the name, 'card'! As if I am going to even attempt to show that to gain entry. Therefore I didn't get into the show and so Stream Creek have paid for me to come to Berlin for nothing. Due to this Joe and I head into Berlin central and do a bit of shopping and soon settle down for beers around 4pm because it's so cold you can't stay out in it for more than 10 minutes at a time. There's snow everywhere and like a true British twat I've only brought my tiny little denim jacket. I

really need to learn that weather in the country I'm leaving is not the same as the weather in the country I am going to. Later on we find a nice exposed brickwork restaurant under a railway bridge and order two nice big juicy steaks and bottle of their finest red wine because, yes, it's all on Stream Creek. After dinner we brave the cold to see what's going on and find ourselves a charming little café type bar adjoined to a small indie cinema. By this time I feel a little bit tipsy and I notice there is super-cute waitress working here. She serves us some drinks and seems to be friendly which is often not the case in Berlin. Many Berliners seem to think it's cool to be cold and indifferent. It's not cool. You just look like a rude, pretentious prick. After the waitress serves us a couple more drinks I start to get the impression that maybe we have a small connection but I'm not quite sure and for some reason I'm not confident enough, or embarrassed to give this information to Joe. I'm starting to become a bit obsessed with her as I often do. I can see that Joe wants to see more of Berlin than just this one bar so I reluctantly agree to go somewhere else. We go outside and it's getting colder so we go into the very next bar we find. It turns out to be a dingy rocker/goth bar and it's not very warm and it's tacky as though it's some sort of ride at Alton Towers. Goths often lack a sense of style. We have one drink and I say 'It's shit here!'
Joe raises his eyebrows and says 'Yep'. Back into the cold we walk for about 10 minutes, struggling to find anything that looks remotely interesting so I say 'Shall we just go back to that first bar?'

'Yeah, why not. I can't be arsed walking around.' Joe replies.

We go back to the bar and I thank the lord that the blonde waitress is still working there. She is dressed all in black. She has skin-tight black jeans on, a little black t-shirt and a pair of black vans on. She is about 5ft.4, has long, naturally curly blonde hair tied up with a pen stuck through a knot at the top. She has a peachy protruding pert little bottom and stands with grace. She has piercing aqua blue/grey eyes, pale white skin and a strong jaw line. A true Aryan Hitler would have approved of. As I may have mentioned before, when I don't know someone and have no good reason to talk to them other than I'm trying to get in their pants I often fail to make contact because I'm not brave enough or I can't think of one damn thing to say or at least nothing that doesn't seem trite or incredibly innocuous that would make me hate myself.

'Hi. You're back.' She says.

'Yeah.' I say a little sheepishly feeling a little foolish and certain she's figured out I'm stalking her.

'Two beers?' she says. Remembering our exciting order from before.

'She's really hot.' I say to Joe.

'Yeah she is.'

I raise this with Joe as it makes me feel as though I'm getting the ball rolling and subsequently building up the nerve to talk to her. I decide I'll talk to her at the next round of drinks. I can feel my heart pounding with anticipation as she approaches.

"After your shift, would you like to join us for a drink?' I think I manage to say this coolly, even though on the inside there's a mass of panic and self-doubt.

'Yeah sure.' She says easily. 'I finish in about an hour.'

'That went better than expected.' I say to Joe.

Over the next hour I do my level best not stare at her and make conversation with Joe but she's all I can think about and what the hell am I going to say to her. I'm pretty drunk now and I am plain awful at inventing chat when I'm drunk and talking to a stranger, especially one that I'm interested in, and if I do think of something to say it's usually some weird plot of how we could kill people and no-one will find out if we feed them to guinea pigs. An hour later, to her word, she joins us and brings us two beers and one for herself.

'So what brings you to Berlin?' she says in her German accent.

'We're here for the Bread & Butter fair.' I reply.

The conversation continues for about half an hour and it was disastrous. I was so boring it hurt. I tell her that I'm here tomorrow night too if she'd like to go for a drink and I give her my number and feel quite shy and daft in doing so. We vacate the premises sharpish after I give her my number because I'm certain she won't call me after that terrible conversation she just had to endure.

'Well that was fucking awful chat! I was quite terrible!'

'Hahaha, yeah! Arhh, it wasn't that bad.' Joe kindly reassures me. I'm not convinced.

'Do you think she'll call me?' I ask.

'Hmmm, not sure about that.' He replies.

The next day we're doing the shops for a bit of research and later in the day a load more

Stream Creek employees join us including one of my ex-girlfriends, Natalie. We trawl around the shops in the freezing cold going from shop to shop in a taxi because we're too frozen to walk more than 30 second down the street. In the early afternoon, to my surprise I get a text from Lena the German waitress. I can't quite believe it after my poor attempt at a conversation the previous night. The down side is she wants to meet for a coffee. A coffee! A bloody coffee! A coffee suggests a very sensible, boring and short encounter and absolutely no possibility of sex.

After we've finished doing the shops we all head back to the hotel. They've all arranged to go out for dinner and then go to some live music bar but clearly and without hesitation I ditch them and head to meet Lena. I can always find them later if it is the dry affair I fear this to be. So I meet her in some local coffee place and we make small talk and it is quite tedious. I'm trying to figure out what's going on. We finish our coffee and I ask if she wants to go for food. She says 'Ya.' We go and get some Thai food and thank the lord she has a God blessed beer. That's a start. I neck mine as I often do unsociably fast and by the time we're finished I've had 3 to her 1. The conversation at this point is going much better and I'm even being almost funny. She asks if I want to go to a little bar that she knows. We hop in cab and turn up at a charming dimly candle lit warm bar with a dark old wooden interior. We settle into a small booth covered in dark red velvety fabric. Lena suggests getting a couple of cocktails and I think, yes, that's the spirit (no pun intended).

She keeps up with me now and we sink the first two and onto the third pretty sharpish. The conversation is gradually getting quite deep and she tells me she was in a 3-way relationship with a girl and a boy and my groin twitches. Lucky bastard! She also tells me about the problems she had with her parents and how they didn't really get on and after a few cocktails she gets a bit teary and I feel a warm glow from the booze and the openness of our conversation and I'm certain I'm in love with her. I of course reason that I'm not, but I could be! Right now I am in love with her even if it is fleeting. Lena invites me back to her place after we realise we're the last ones in the bar and they're hinting for us to leave. It's now 3am. We get in a cab and 15 minutes later we stop and at that point I realise I don't know where I am and that I'm supposed to meet everyone in the morning at 9am. Oh well fuck it. It's not like this kind of thing happens every day.
We walk up her communal creaky old wooden stairs up to the second floor and into her flat. It's probably at least 60 years old and has a certain charm. We head into her bedroom and it's a solid quirky girl's abode. High ceilings, bits of art she's done laying around the place and a nice soft perfumed white bed and old sash windows with bits of jewellery hanging off the latches. Even though we're here I still don't know for sure if we're going to fuck or not. I take off my boots in anticipation anyway and climb onto her very close to floor mattress laid on top of wooden pallets. She climbs on top of me and we start to kiss passionately and soon enough we're stripping each other. She has a tiny perfectly formed body and she fits me perfectly. Her breasts are very pert

and still a handful. Her waist is tiny and
her butt is curvaceous. I remove her bra.
I've got reasonably good at this from
practice. I take her nipple in my mouth
whilst she straddles me although I'm still
not inside her. She then takes my cock
firmly in her hand and wraps her mouth
around it. I remember the grip she had on my
cock so well. Holding it so firmly in in her
small hands whilst she sucked my dick. It
really felt like she knew what she was
doing. Taking control of my cock and working
her tongue over it perfectly. It was almost
too good and I didn't want it to be all over
before we fucked. I laid her onto her back.
She had a pure white landing strip proving
she really was the genuine article. She
looked so hot I couldn't believe I was about
to put my cock in her. I held her legs apart
and played with her clit with the end of my
cock until she pulled me into her. I pushed
my cock very slowly, a bit at a time inside
her cunt and it was as firm as was her grip.
It felt divine. It felt as though my dick
belonged in there and should stay for an
eternity. She was as horny as hell and was
upping the tempo to quite a pace and I was
happy to oblige her. At one point she was
pulling a face and squirming and her pussy
was pretty tight so I thought I was hurting
her but then she let out a gasp and I
realised this was her cum face. Once she had
cum it allowed me to really give it to her
in the way that I wanted to, so then I could
bring myself to orgasm and it didn't take
long before I was cumming hard inside her.
Fuck, she turned me on something bad. Soon
after she curled up, her back and bum
towards me with my arms wrapped around her
and soon enough I fell into a wondrous cloud
dwelling like sleep.

Beep! Beep! Beep! Beep! BeeP!
'Fucck!' I had somehow managed to remember to set my alarm it was about 7.45am and with about 3 hours sleep I was feeling fucking horrendous. Here I was laid in one of the most comfortable, warm beds with this tiny pert ass teasing my hard cock. It was hard before I'd even woken up. You never know whether they're going to go for morning sex but I thought, hell I've got to try. She was the perfect host and guided my cock inside her from behind whilst in the spooning position. It feels amazing and I know this is going to be a quickie and it fucking needs to be because I don't know where I am or how to get back to the hotel. It's over in about 5 minutes and she moans with relative content and says 'Don't go.'
'You've no idea how much I really don't want to go.' I tell her. I reluctantly get out of her warm bed into her cold room and put on last night's clothes and feel like a right dirt bag. Lena tells me I should just be able to get a cab in the street. I give her a long single kiss and say my goodbyes. I feel like I'm still connected to her and it hurts me to leave her but I feel like I will see her again somehow. I actually do see her again 6 months later and it all goes terribly wrong but that's another story. I leave the block and enter the street where it's even colder than before and there's a good foot of snow and I'm still wearing my pathetic little denim jacket, what a tit! There are no taxis to be seen in any direction and I feel as though I'm in the middle of nowhere. I choose a direction to walk in that I think will give me a better chance of getting cab and 15 minutes later it's apparent that I'm very wrong.

It's now 8.15am. I run back in the other direction for 10 minutes, which isn't any more convincing and I'm thinking I'm completely fucked here. How the fuck am I going to get home? I persevere, fast walking in this new direction certain I'm going to die of exposure. I can barely feel my wet feet or face. Another 10 minutes pass and I see a cab about 100 metres away and leg it after it. I bang on the taxi window like someone desperate for aid. I tumble into the joyous warmth of the taxi and I momentarily fall in love with the bearded German Father Xmas cab driver. When my brain cells thaw out I don't love him anymore but I'm still eternally grateful to him. We get to the hotel 11 minutes later, I look at my watch and I've got about a quarter of an hour to get ready. I run into the hotel hoping no one from Stream Creek is sitting in the lobby early and catches me coming in like a dirty stop-out, also because I don't want Natalie to know either. I'm not a complete bastard and that would be rather awkward. Little did I know that in the future the bitch would get together with one of my mates at Stream Creek. There's just no honour amongst some people. Luckily there was no one in the lobby. I jump in the shower, clean my teeth, change my pants, socks and t-shirt and somehow in about 20 minutes I'm ready and feel like a new-ish man. I come down stairs to the lobby where some folk are waiting but not all and I say, 'Morning all!' like nothing had ever happened.

Anyway, back to the present.
The lad and the chubby girl who's names I forgot the second they told me, both decline my offer of a late drink as they're tired. I

always fancy a drink when I get off a flight. Camille says, appearing in an innocent way to her friends, 'Oui. I am not tired.'
We drop her friends off at their place and continue to mine. We have a couple of glasses of wine and it's not long until we're both stark naked and screwing on my sofa. 91.
The next night I meet up with one of my old familiar sex friends and she stays the night. In the morning we head out for breakfast and I have my arm around her and who do I see coming the other way but Camille. I clock her a good distance away before she sees me so I just keep my head down and hope she doesn't see me. It's quite busy in the street so I might get away with it. I catch a glimpse of her in my peripheral vision and she appears to be looking at her phone and doesn't see me. Phew! That could have been uncomfortable for all three of us. One minute later I get a text. 'I see you!'

x Table sleeping x

Back at Stream Creek on a Thursday a week later Mark my manager tells me that he heard on the grapevine there's a girl in the women's wear department that mentioned she fancied me in a meeting. He describes what she looks like and I know exactly whom he is referring to and I'm excited about it. She is hot and I've noticed her around although we've never spoken. Her name I discover is Lara. She is 22, slim, has long dark brown hair with blonde dip-dyed tips. She is very pale but it suits her. She pretty much only wears black and has her septum pierced. She looks a tiny bit gothic but without all the tacky make-up. She has the face of a model but doesn't know it. Her face is defined and angular but still soft looking. I find her slightly pointy small nose and full Eastern European looking lips incredibly attractive. She is virtually perfect to me.
Like a gutless teenager I email her rather than just go and talk to her in case it's just a load of Chinese whispers. I email her to say 'a little bird told me…'
'Told you what?' She replies.
'That perhaps you might be interested in me?'
'Oh sorry, no!' She replies.
Quickly followed by another email saying, 'Only joking.'
I like it. It's a good start. A girl that's attractive and has a good sense of humour can be hard to find. Very hard! Attractive girls tend to forget that they need to have a personality because the world just hands itself to them on plate and they feed on it hungrily, forgetting that there's anyone else at the table.

I ask her if she wants to meet up later and she agrees.

I'm as excited as a child on Christmas Eve. I fancy her a great deal and even more so now that I have discovered she has a personality too.

We meet at the Tate Modern. Culture is always a good way of impressing a girl although a bit pretentious, I'll admit. It would have been even more impressive if it had have been open. Bad start to the date but she doesn't seem bothered and finds it funny. I like her. We chat a bit about having seen each other around at work and which other people at Stream Creek we both know. Because I'm a classy bastard I take her to Pizza Express in Liverpool Street. Another reason for this is because it's closer to my flat. If you want a better chance of getting laid then you need to ensure the logistics are in your favour and it doesn't give the girl enough time to change her mind or sober up. I like Pizza Express. The food is good and it's cheap. No messing around. Also, I love the dough balls they do with the garlic butter. Absolute beauties. Two of my favourite things in the world, bread and butter. What's not to like. I order a bottle of white wine for us to share and we both tuck in to eagerly. We are talking fluidly with plenty of interspersions of laughter. She looks so beautiful over the candlelight. She tells me about how her Dad is a potter and how positive he always is. I am happy for her and jealous at the same time.

We finish our pizzas and dough balls and what's left of the second bottle of white wine. We're both feeling jovial and it seems to be going swimmingly and we're both quite tipsy by this point. I suggest we go and

have a drink at the Ten Bells pub up the
road opposite Spitalfields market.
'What would you like to drink?' I ask.
'A pint of Guinness please.' Lara says.
Guinness! It just keeps getting better. A
hot girl with a personality who drinks
pints, and pints of Guinness at that! We
chat for a bit longer and finish our pints
fairly quickly and she's starting to look a
bit drunk now. We go outside for a
cigarette, which we both rolled ourselves.
Another thing I like about her. We're still
getting on well and she's looking at me with
soft pretty piercing green eyes and I think
maybe this is the time to kiss her. We are
already standing quite close to one another.
I look into her eyes to gauge whether she is
inviting me to kiss her and I decide that
she is. I move in to kiss her and thank the
lord she reciprocates and kisses me back.
Her lips feel like perfection. She does not
disappoint in the kissing area. It's such an
important thing that when you kiss someone
it fits just so. I think if you kiss someone
and it doesn't feel quite right you should
just nip it in the bud right there and then.
We head back into the pub and she buys
another round and that one goes down fairly
sharpish too. I get us another round after
the last one's done and return to the table.
I sit down and I'm talking to her and I
realise after a minute that she's not
responding. I thought she was just looking
down at something, perhaps her phone, when I
realise that she has actually nodded off.
Shit! I bored her to sleep. It would seem
that the heavy pints of Guinness have put
her into a booze-induced coma. 'Hey!' I say
and she jolts up quickly, looking like she
doesn't know where she is.

'Come on,' I say and help her up. I've not seen such a sudden change of state in quite some time.
'Hey mate, do you want this pint, it's not been touched?' I say to an older guy at the bar.
'Thanks.' He says slightly suspiciously as people often do if offered a free drink that's already been poured.
The two older fellas sitting at the bar smile humorously seeing my situation and I just raise my eyebrows, acknowledging my predicament to them.
I take Lara outside in her dazed state and hail down a black cab. I open up the cab door and help her in. She sleeps on my shoulder the whole way home. When we get into my flat I show her to my bedroom and she gets into bed fully clothed. I go into the kitchen and poor myself a glass of scotch, sit down on the sofa in the lounge and put my feet up on the table and light up a rollie. When I go to bed she is fast asleep and I lie next to her and soon drift off myself.
Lara and I have now been seeing each other for about three weeks and there has been zero sexual activity other than dry humping whilst fully clothed which is shit. Despite my sexual frustrations I rather like that she is making me wait. It shows a real sign of dignity on her part and I fancy her more than ever. One night after a movie and a few drinks we are kissing as we often do but this time she is allowing me to remove her clothes. To say I'm excited is an understatement. Eventually we are both naked but something doesn't feel quite right. I keep kissing and rubbing up against her however she is a bit stationary. I open her legs and play with her with my fingers for a

bit. I can't read her at all. I think
perhaps she is just not that experienced in
the bedroom or not quite comfortable or
lacking in confidence a bit which is
surprising. We start to fuck but it's all
wrong. I feel like I'm fucking a mannequin,
or like it's rape but there is something
darkly sinister and carnal about that kind
of sex. I actually cum quite quickly because
I can see there's no chance of her cumming
so I just get on with it. It just felt so
awkward. It doesn't make sense. When we kiss
it's perfect and we have a lot in common.
Maybe it's just because it's the first time.
Over the following weeks the sex doesn't get
any better and I also discover that she
can't suck dick for toffee. There's a
presence of teeth, discomfort and mild
bruising. She's not got any idea of what to
do with a cock. Maybe her last boyfriend
didn't like head or just gave up on her in
fear she might bite the end of his dick off.
As usual I start to find flaws in what I
previously found flawless. She doesn't
really have any tits, which I originally
didn't mind as she is slim and it was
proportionate but now whenever I see a girl
with a good rack I ache for some of that
action. Secondly I've noticed that her upper
arms are actually a bit flabby and hairier
than I like. This is something I generally
do not like in women, bingo wings. I like a
bit of tone in women's arms. I don't mean a
gym-mentalist but a little bit of muscle is
nice. You know, so you look like you could
climb a tree. I don't really want to date
someone who looks as though they couldn't
escape out of a window if there's a fire. So
here begins our relationship's fast demise.
I just can't stop looking at the tops of her
arms now and the sex is terrible. It's the

worst sex I've ever had with the person I probably fancied the most. Fuck! After a few weeks of this dead, missing connection sex, I know we mustn't be right for each other and I call it off. Back to the drawing board! 92.

x When the Moon hits your eye x

"When the Moon hits your eye like a bigger piece of pie, that's amore", has to be conceivably the most inane and irritating lyric I've possibly ever heard. Our band are working our arses off to try and get a foot in the music industry door and some cunt is singing about moons and pies in your fucking eyes. What a cunt! That's why I don't like Italy! Italy is one of the most overrated countries in the world. They're about a decade behind the UK culturally. Their government has to be one of the most corrupt in Europe. I mean Berlusconi is their prime minister. Who were the other candidates? Satan, The God Father and Gaddafi. No one seems to pay tax in Italy so the greedy fuckers have gone bankrupt. It serves them right for voting for that baldy sex pest. Everyone seems to rave about Italian food and I can honestly say when I was there it was the most average food I've had the misfortune to taste. They're so patriotically arrogant, the only food you can get in Italy, is Italian and every restaurant seems to serve the same fucking dish. Rome, however, I didn't mind when our band went to play there. We had a blast.

Anyway, I'm travelling to Italy for work, and it's on a weekend. Balls! It's a bi-yearly shoe fair. It is, to be fair to it, set in a picturesque little town called Riva Del Garda, which has cobbled streets and beautiful old architecture. There are a few of us travelling to Italy together. There's my assistant buyer who is attractive but stupid and also the kid's buying/design team. We do a day's work walking round the fair, attending meetings, which is all very boring. It's usually a good piss-up when we go out and it starts well. We finish at the fair around 3pm and the sun is shining and it's pretty warm so when we get to the hotel we change into our swimming gear and sit around the pool drinking bottled beers. One of the design managers Abby is pretty cool. We got on well last time we came but she had a boyfriend then and come to think of it she still does, but the relationship is on the ropes now. Apart from Tanya she is the only person on the trip I'd socialise with outside of this situation.

Tanya decides she wants to paint my toenails. I already have quite dainty feet so the addition of baby pink nail polish makes them look very lady like indeed. I don't mind her doing my nails, it's just another excuse to be touched in some way. It's not a turn-on for me it's just nice being touched. Sometimes when I go through airport security I don't take my belt off so the alarm goes off and somebody has to frisk me. I always seem to get the fat sweaty guy though which isn't so enjoyable. I never seem to get the sexy lady human.

When the sun goes down we go and get changed and then head out into the town. We go and find a restaurant that has outside seating so that we can smoke. We order dinner and it's worse than average. We do have a pretty funny conversation, mostly slagging off other people from Stream Creek and playing the game called 'Fuck, marry or push off a cliff.' The giant baby seems to be finding himself tumbling to his death rather a lot in this game, unsurprisingly. After a while I change the subject of the game from humans to animals.

I start the suggestions with 'Duck, dog…'
'I'd definitely fuck the dog!' Tanya blurts out without a thought.
'I haven't even given you all the options yet and you just pretty much announced that you'd fuck a dog!' I said.
This then earns Tanya the nickname of The Garda Dog Fucker. We all get pretty pissed over the evening and head back to the hotel around 2am. I'm walking back with Abby and I feel like something could happen but I'm not sure as she is still technically in a relationship even if it is nearing the end. We were doing a bit handholding underneath the table. That has to mean she's into me right? I suppose that shows the level of my insecurity or fear of rejection that I'm still not sure. Of course she must. You don't hold hands under the table if you just want to be friends but when it's happening to you, you don't always recognise it. We have a couple of drinks in the lobby and I make my excuses and go to my room. I surreptitiously text Abby my room number and hope that she follows. 10 minutes later there's a knock on the door. She has a slightly sheepish but naughty look on her face and as soon as the door's closed we start kissing. She's a good kisser. In no time we're both naked and I'm in between her legs and we're having good old-fashioned messy drunken sex. When I'm going to cum she takes me in her mouth. Damn it's hot when that happens. After a few beers and smokes she goes back to her own room so not to create any suspicion.
The next night we're out again and the gang all want to go out the local club when it gets to midnight but the place is a dive. It's full of 50-year-old euro men on their rare annual night out in their dodgy over-

designed jeans and terrible shirts and tacky shoes, dancing like it's 1985. It's not! It's a regular sausage party and the few girls in there get swarmed upon.
It's around 1am so we let them fuck off to the club and Abby and I make our way back to the hotel once more. On the way I say, 'I'd like to fuck you in that church!'
'Me too!' She says and runs over to check if the doors are open. I was being a bit of an over-confident tit, not thinking she would actually act on it. When she did I slightly panicked. The doors were locked and I breathed a sigh of relief. We continue to walk and then she drags me down a side street and says 'I want you to fuck me here.' The street is very dark but there are still people passing and anyone caring to look could easily see us. For some reason we get pretty much completely naked rather than just pulling my cock out through my flies. She bends over and leans against the wall with the palms of her hands and I fuck her from behind. It's great fun but I'm a bit drunk and can't really cum from it. We fuck for a bit and then put our clothes back on and go back to the hotel and finish the job off properly. This time she stays the night and in the morning gives me an amazing blowjob. Maybe Italy's not so bad. 93.

x I'm sick x

I texted Stream Creek on Monday morning
having returned from Italy and said 'I'm not
coming in today, I don't feel well.'
The office manager Miranda Elliot (a fat,
saggy, old, miserable, desperately needs a
good fuck but facially looks like the goofy
Gremlin from Gremlins 2 and who wants to
fuck that?) replies, 'What's wrong?'
'I don't feel well.'
'Yes, but what's wrong?' She says.
'I don't feel well'.
'But why exactly?'
'I'M NOT WELL!!'
'You need to tell me why?'
'Are you a doctor?
'No'.
'Then mind your own business you old goat-
fucker!!'
Unsurprisingly I didn't return to Stream
Creek after that.

x I'm free x

So now I have the day off. Well, an indefinite amount of days off. Hmmm, what to do with it? I haven't seen Izzie in a while as I have been making excuses that I have been busy with work engagements. One thing it's always good to do is to keep at least two to three women on the back burner for when you need sex or sometimes just for company… but mostly for sex.
I text Izzie and she says she's free. I'm in that kind of mood. Thinking about it gives an erection and that decided it for me. Izzie is free because she quit her job in marketing or something like that and is attempting to become an actress. This seems as unlikely to happen as my attempt to be a full-time musician. I've seen videos of her and I think she's okay but I can't really tell. When you know someone it just seems like they're doing a bad impression of someone else. Either that's the case or she just isn't that good at it.
Izzie is about the same height as me and has a curvy body in a very sexual and womanly way. She has decent-sized breasts, browned skin like a Brazilian and has long dark straight hair. She is actually a mix of Japanese and Italian, I think. Hybrids often do look the most attractive. She has a very slight Japanese look to her eyes and pair of full Italian lips. A real hottie! The only downside is when she smiles there's a tiny bit too much gum but then that's me being pedantic. I can find fault in diamond. I really don't like that about myself. It's not that I think I'm perfect, I really don't. There are loads of things wrong with

me both mentally and aesthetically. I just
do my best to ignore them. I can't seem to
ignore it when certain small things turn me
off and then it just escalates from fancying
the hell out of someone to not fancying them
at all anymore and not wanting to fuck the
person you previously didn't even think you
could fuck.
I head over to Izzie's in Kentish Town. It's
a miserable out so we've planned a day
watching films on her bed. She lives in a
Victorian terrace. It's nice but rough
around the edges and not very well taken
care of. This is the state of nearly all
house/flat shares in London. Property owners
& estate agents in London are a bunch of
uncaring, greedy pricks. There should be a
standard. It's not as if it's cheap either.
I don't know how these bastards get away
with it. There should be a union! Maybe
there is?
I knock on the thick blue paint chipped
door. The door opens.
'Hi!' she says.
'Hi back.' I reply. She sort of laugh
smiles, where you snort air out of your
nostrils. I follow her in.
'Tea?' she asks.
'Lovely.' I reply.
I observe her living room. There's a few
70's music posters on the wall that look as
though they may well be from that actual
era. There's some wooden box shelving with
various books and records left by random
residents over the years.
'Sugar?' Izzie calls out.
'Yes please.' I call back.
Izzie brings the tea into the room and then
motions me up to her room with her head and
eyes. I follow her up the stairs whilst
looking at her arse and thinking about the

fact that I've seen that arse naked and been inside her vagina. The thing with sex is that it's a bit like pain. You know that there was a distinct feeling when it happened but you can't recall how it feels exactly. It's when you actually put your cock inside a woman, there's that feeling of 'aaaaaah.., that's what it feels like' and that's why I spend so much time chasing it and thinking about it and wanting to fuck every woman that's remotely attractive. Every fuck is different and exciting though some can be shit but even the shit ones are good in some ways.

We go into her room and it's fairly small and definitely a girl's room. It has that smell of perfume and cosmetics but there's no pink in sight. Pink can make you feel like a paedophile, like you're in a child's bedroom. We settle onto her bed, a soft double bed with white covers. She pulls her 15-inch white Mac out and says, 'What do you fancy?'

'I don't mind, what have you got?'

We settle on *'Lars and the real girl'*.

At this point I hadn't seen anything with the mono-expression wielding Ryan Gosling and I quite liked him in it. It's about a social retard that orders one of these full-size lady sex dolls that looks disturbingly like a real person. I can't say I wouldn't. I may not make it all the way through this film, as new sexual pairings often don't, so after I've finished my tea I slip off into the bathroom for a piss. The last thing you want when you're getting down to it is to be thinking about how much you need to urinate. There are black mould spots on the white walls and ceiling in the bathroom. This again is a common occurrence and another example of estate agents' and property

owners' malpractice. I make a mental note of this. 'How do we get even?'
There's so much crap in here, about twice the amount of toothbrushes than the amount of current residents. There are various old hair products with weird brown stains on them arranged around the dirty bath. I finish pissing, wash my hands and look around for something to dry them on but I don't fancy the look of any of the filthy rags they call towels hanging around. I dry them on my jeans and return to Izzie's room. We continue to watch the movie lying down on the bed with her head on my chest and her hand on my leg. I can feel my cock starting to twitch and I'm quickly losing concentration in the film. She cranes her neck slightly to look up at me and I lean towards her and we kiss each other on the lips. She has warm, soft but firm lips and is a good kisser. She turns over to face me and climbs on top of me. She leans down to kiss me but not fully. She holds her mouth above mine just slightly out of reach, to tease me. I don't mind this sometimes, if you really fancy the person it's quite fun but when you're with someone that you really don't fancy that much you're just thinking for fuck's sake, give it a rest and get on with it. She lowers down and we kiss with just our lips. We then begin to kiss open-mouthed with our tongues deep inside each other's mouth. I like deep, full, passionate kissing like this. Both types are good though. I find that when you kiss someone and you never really get into that full passionate, open-mouthed, tongue penetration, it always feels non-committal and as if you're not fully engaged. Izzie then gives me this look like she's about to make my day and starts to slide down towards

the fun area of my anatomy. She starts to pull at my belt buckle. It's hard to explain the excitement you feel when this happens. No matter how many girls have done this I still get jittery just thinking about it! She undoes my belt and tugs my jeans down. My excitement is evident by the pre-cum on my pants or briefs or whatever you might call them. I occasionally feel embarrassed about the pre-cum on my pants. God knows why. Maybe it's that it shows too much excitement or that it means that they have your cum in their mouth as soon as they have begun and some girls don't like it when you cum in their mouth. Frigid cows. Us men stick our tongues into their sweaty, bloody, discharge-ridden vaginas and don't complain about it. You've got to get into oral sex fully or don't bother doing it at all. I think that when you no longer have an interest in giving your girl/boyfriend oral then you know you don't really fancy them that much anymore. Once when I was driving back from a kung-fu lesson with my then girlfriend, she gave me a blow-job whilst I drove and when I came in her mouth she wound down the window and spat it out of the car, delightful….though still quite sexy. Maybe not for the car behind us!

Izzie peels off my underwear and pulls them down to my ankles. I use my feet to fully remove my jeans and pants. I don't like shagging or having my cock sucked with them still on. I feel restricted and I don't like being straight legged whilst it happens, I like to open my legs when I'm being sucked off.

Izzie looks at me once more before lowering her eyes towards my hard dick and she runs the tip of her tongue along the end of my cock and into and around the slit, clearly

unperturbed by the pre-cum. A good start!
She rolls her tongue around my bell-end a
few more times before taking the whole of my
cock into her mouth. This feels fucking
amazing!! A good blowjob is as rare as
rocking horse shit. She builds up a rhythm
and I'm already starting to feel on edge.
She is getting a little faster and also
stroking my balls with her nails and I can
feel I'm going to cum. I normally make an
announcement of this but it takes me off
guard and before I know it I'm cumming into
her mouth which seems to also take her by
surprise but she swallows it like a pro.
That has to be one the quickest and most
successful blowjobs I've had in a long time.
I'm lying there enjoying the afterglow and
she goes and ruins it by saying,
'You weren't supposed to cum yet,' which
makes me feel guilty as she obviously wanted
me to fuck her.
'You can't say that. You shouldn't have
sucked my cock so well. You're ruining the
enjoyment of it now.'
She pulls a face of slight annoyance and
confusion but then smiles.
'Oh sorry, I… I just… wanted to fuck you
that's all'.
'Give it ten.' I say.
I pull my pants on and we resume watching
the film whilst she swills down my cum with
the remainder of what's left of her cup of
tea. When the film finishes and I'm
restocked, I keep my promise and give her a
good fucking, missionary style with her legs
wrapped around me and I cum once more. I'm
not quite sure if she came or not but she
seemed to enjoy it. If she did cum it wasn't
obvious but one thing I've learnt over the
years is, don't ask!

x Are you mugging me off? X

Are you mugging me off? Or 'Are you taking
my mug?' as my French friend Pascaline said
to me when she tried to repeat the phrase,
having not understood the idiom. To be fair
it doesn't make much sense to me either.
It's mid-April and the band has the second
round of the competition coming up tonight.
It's a Thursday, supposedly the new Friday.
I think that's because it's another excuse
to obliterate your brain and go back into
work on Friday morning, numb to the reality
of the job and life you loathe. We've been
trying to promote the gig as much as
possible on the usual social media sites
that drain the very life and spirit out of
you and annoy the fuck out of all your
friends.

I head out of the flat early in morning
around 7am. I've got my dark grey jeans
rolled up at the bottom and I'm wearing dark
red derby doc shoes, white socks, black crew
neck t-shirt and a vintage blue denim
jacket, collar up. As I walk along the
quiet street, I see a couple of guys walking
in front of me and there's also a woman
walking towards them. They look like a pair
of road shift workers who've recently
clocked off and maybe had a can or two
already but not completely drunk. The guy on
the left looks fairly regular and normal in
his work gear just walking along however the
guy on the right has dirty overalls falling
down, a dirty white vest and rigger boots
and also a push bike and is shouting at the
top of his voice at any random passers-by
with idiotic commentary. He's clearly after
attention because he hates himself and is

trying to impress his mate with his foolish audacity. I can see that the woman approaching them is nervous and inevitably he makes some sort of derogatory comment towards her. This is in my top 5 pet hates. I fucking hate it when men shout out at women or letch at them to the point that they feel threatened. They seem to think it's fine to just go up to a woman and say, 'Hey baby! You wanna fuck?'
In what universe has any woman ever said, 'Hey, yeah. You know what? I do want to fuck you seeing as you put it so sweetly.'
So why do they say it? They're fucking animals and should be treated as such. It seems that 9 times out of 10 in London it's black men. Why is this?
The guy giving out the abuse in this instance is in fact black or possibly mixed race. The woman walks straight past them keeping her head down to avoid any trouble or further ridicule. My blood is boiling at this point.
I am walking at a faster pace than the two morons and know that at this rate I am going to have to overtake them. I consider slowing down to avoid the aggravation but I think, no, fuck them, and continue at my normal speed. As I pass them they are distracted and I can feel my heart pumping waiting to see if the dickhead notices me. He does.
'Oi! Nice white socks!' He shouts at me. 'I used to have a pair of those in the 80's'. He says, sniggering to his mate. 'I'm real trendy I am.' He claims.
I turn as I'm walking, give him a look and say, 'Yeah, I can see that.'
He gets all excited and nearly drops his bike as though he's about to pounce on me and he says 'Oi! You northern monkey!' He says. I'm not even from the north. I'm from

Leicester you prick. I can't believe I'm suffering racial abuse in my own country! 'I'd fuckin'… I'd… I'd fuckin' do you if it weren't for these security cameras.' He shouts.
His mate doesn't look like he's up for this and I think this black guy is clearly mentally deranged and even though I don't reckon it will be me versus the two of them I'm not feeling confident enough to know I'm going to win this fight. I haven't even had that many fights and not all of them successful. I'm fucking furious however and I can feel my blood coming to the surface. Why should we normal people, just trying to make our way in life have to be terrorised by these illiterate, uneducated, misanthropic, idiotic, fucking Nazis. I decide not to react and I keep walking. All I wanted was to get some bread and milk.
I can't let this go and I can't stop thinking about it. I'm not having this. This is my damn street and all those poor women who have to put up with this crap must be sick to the back teeth of it. I head into the nearest corner shop I see. I have a look around, pick up what I need and pay the Turkish guy in the shop who barely acknowledges my existence whilst talking on his mobile. I see the two guys are ahead of me now on the other side of the street and they say their goodbyes and head off in separate directions. The black guy heads off into the park. I cross the road and I follow him into the park. The street is still quiet other than the odd bit of traffic. I'm following him from a reasonable distance as to not appear to be following him, just as though I'm crossing through park like anyone else. The idiot has of course shut his trap now that he no longer has an audience. His

attention is taken by scrolling though his phone whilst simultaneously pushing his bike. I follow him through the winding paths of the park. It's completely empty other than some homeless guy asleep on one of benches. The guy approaches a section of the park where there's a low wooden, flat bridge about 4 feet off the ground crossing a shallow section of dirty pond water and it is without railings. I put down the groceries I bought onto the nearest bench. The guy stops on the bridge to write a text and he's sniggering to himself. He's probably texting some hopeless slag that's just sent him a dirty picture. He's engrossed in what he's doing and doesn't notice me coming towards him. When I'm 5 meters away I burst into a run. He is putting most of his weight onto his bike and is the other side of it and is only a foot away from the edge of the bridge. Just as I'm about to make contact he looks up and blurts out, 'Ay!'

With all my force I kick out at the thickest part of the bike frame. He is forced backwards, looses his balance and steps back into thin air and his bike follows him into the stinking pond water. Without hesitation, I jump down to the side of him. It's only about one or two feet of water but that's enough. Before the guy has chance to move and with the benefit of the bike now being on top of him, I take my right foot and force it down onto the front of his neck crushing his oesophagus. He is convulsing and panicking and thrashing around like an alligator trying to get a hand free to remove my leg. His other arm is trapped below the bike and with my other foot I restrain his other arm but the guy is still pretty strong. He doesn't give up and he keeps trying to budge me but the combined weight and the fact my shoe is crushing his neck is too much for him. His head is tilted back under the force of my shoe and what glimpses I see of his face show a great strain. He begins to weaken and his escape attempts are now less frequent and with a sign of resignation and I'm quietly singing 'Don't fence me' with my teeth clenched. I am looking down on him although it is difficult to see through the dirty water. Once there is no longer any movement I wait for a further 20 seconds to make sure, which feels like a lifetime. Meanwhile I'm looking around me to check there's no one else around. I don't see anyone other than through the bushes on the other side, in the open grassy park area I see a murder of crows. How ironic.

I remove my shoe from his neck, step back and spit on the dead prick. 'How do you like my socks now dickhead?'

I climb out onto the bridge and the bottom half of my jeans are soaked and filthy. I go to the blue flimsy plastic bag containing my groceries and retrieve two cans of larger. I open one can of larger, climb back down into the pond and poor it around the dead prick. I then throw the empty can to the side of him. The kind of distance it may have travelled had he have fallen in whilst riding his bike. I take the unopened can and put it into his overalls pocket. With his phone floating around next to him, that just adds to the effect and so it's clearly not a mugging so there's no need for further investigation. Another obnoxious waster laid to rest. See ya!

x It's an idiom!... You're an idiot! x

'Hello chaps,' I say to the band.
'How do!' Andy replies.
'How arrre ya maaate' says Johnny. He isn't
Australian. It's just something we imitate
from something we saw on a Russell Brand
programme once. This is when I still liked
Russell Brand. I think he should've stuck to
comedy. Although he makes some interesting
points politically, and I agree with much of
what he has to say, his motives seem
questionable and it seems disingenuous to me
and another reason for him to attract
attention to himself.
'Alright,' says Chris, in his friendly way.
We all give each other a hug. We always
greet each other this way. Re-affirming our
bond like a returning penguin mother from a
long day's fishing. We are all around the
same age and a similar height and build
weirdly. We're all adorned in skinny jeans,
t-shirts and leather jackets. Who says we
aren't individuals? We didn't start off this
way. We all looked completely different at
the beginning and over time amalgamated into
one single entity. For example, when we met
Johnny (the drummer) he had tattoos and the
others had none. Now, we are all covered in
tattoos like it's a competition. Chris
stopped at 3, however. Chris is a fairly
quiet lad, with a certain amount of OCD but
still gets very much involved in the band
banter. I think he's a genuinely kind
person, probably the nicest and most
positive out of the 4 of us - though Andy
and I are fairly miserable people. Chris
also has a tattoo on his wrist that spells
his name in Elvish. He has short brown-fair

and is also a shoe designer which is how this all got started.

Andy is the bassist in the band. He is a building site supervisor but doesn't really fit the stereotype you might imagine. He and Chris grew up together so they've been best mates for years. He has shaved ginger hair and a big homeless-style beard. Andy is also fairly quiet and relatively reserved but, like Chris, when we're all together we tend to get pretty excited and a tad rowdy. This usually involves us taking our clothes off and dancing on tables. Andy is the opposite of Chris. He is not a positive person but not a bad one either. He rather enjoys wallowing in his miserable demeanour and projection and he never smiles on stage, though I know deep down he couldn't be happier and there's no place he'd rather be.

Johnny is always in a pretty good mood for a drummer. He has a generally optimistic outlook on life although sometimes he's unrealistically optimistic, especially when it comes to time. Seeing as he is the person that is supposed to keep time in the band, he is the one who is always late. Only Johnny can claim to be 'just around the corner' in his van and still take over an hour to arrive. Johnny has long shoulder-length ginger hair. He has the most tattoos and a dangling cross earring in his left ear. He works with his dad in their own building company so he has that slightly cracked worker look about his hands, which are covered in two black rose tattoos. If the lads were to describe me they'd probably say I was a narcissistic, egomaniacal, sex pest, and have small hands. I often wonder if I ever show my softer to side to them. Sometimes I think I'm always putting on a performance but I'm not being disingenuous.

This is me being me. It's just a more excited and/or moody version. You can't have your ups without your downs. It's not as though I'm just going to blurt out that I was crying last night and I desperately wish I had someone that I loved and they loved me. One just doesn't announce those things out of context.

Our gig tonight is at Dingwalls in Camden. We carry our stuff up the cobbled street towards the venue, which is situated near the food market and the canal there. It's busy all around with a mixture of tourists and the local punks sitting around on the bridge drinking lager out of cans and trying to look tough, taking a pound off any tourist who wants to take a snap of them. They look out-dated and comedic to me, as though they've been paid by the council to decorate the place and give it some authenticity like when you get fellas dressed as Roman soldiers outside of ancient coliseums.

We go into the entrance of the venue and there is no one in the joint other than the bar staff, the sound engineer and the promoter. Fucking promoters. They are quite possibly the ones to blame for destroying the music scene in London. They don't give a toss who plays, or how good the band are, as long as you can bring 10 or more people to a gig. It completely kills peoples' belief in turning up to a random venue and there being great bands playing so all it creates is a mass of apathy, so the only people you end up playing to are your mates and the other bands' mates.

Probably the worst thing about being in a band is the waiting. One thing I've learnt over time is, fuck sound checks! They can get a decent level after your first song and

it's better than getting there for sound
check and then having to wait for six hours
before you play.

'Have you ever fucked a pig?' I ask Johnny.

'Err.' Johnny says thinking about the
question with a grin on his face.

'Chris has definitely shagged someone that
looked like a pig.' Andy interjects and we
all laugh.

The place fills right up and there's about
150 or so people in the venue now.

Most of our usual gang turn up to see us
play. We've accumulated a delightful group
of friends over the last few years. There
are some friends from work, ex-girlfriends,
other girls I'm currently sleeping with or
have recently slept with which adds a bit of
tension and none of those girls speak to
each other as they are not friends as such.
I think they just death stare each other
from a distance. Johnny's brothers and
sister are here too. A very charming set of
siblings. John and Julia are here too. They
are two of my favourite people in the world.
They are both in their early forties. They
are both smart and loving, and they both
behave like anarchic children. Especially
after a few drinks!

The first band goes on and they're not too
bad. A fairly standard unoriginal indie band
but the songs are well written and their
performance is pretty tight. The second band
go on stage and they are an odd collection
with some goth girl singing with a gaggle of
losers who all fancy her and have no sign of
any talent.

We're next up. I always get quite tense and
serious before I go on stage and rush around
even though I want to look as though I'm as
cool as a cucumber. As soon as I'm setup,

tuned and have my guitar resting in my hands I'm settled.

'Hello.' I say to the room. 'We're The Winter Kicks. We're here to play you some songs. That's why we're here….and this is one of them.'

We kick off with a song called Buddies, a delightful song about fuck buddies. What a surprise.

The gig goes down a storm and the crowd seem to love it so we're feeling pretty good about it when we're done. As I said it's a ridiculous voting system so who knows what's going to happen but we get a decent show of hands. How the frick can anyone properly count that amount of hands that are sticking up at a gig when there's a hundred or so people. What if it's the difference between one or two votes? As if they've properly counted them all. Nonetheless, we do go through to the next round, having come second to a Japanese band who to be fair were pretty good and sounded relatively original.

We all get pretty fucked up after the bands are done and after half an hour of the DJ spinning records we get all our mates together and the remaining crowd and even some of the other bands up and dancing on the furniture. It's a great night and everyone's pissed up and having a ball. The DJ is playing great guitar band type music and knows his audience. I'm getting a few looks in my direction from Izzie, Jessie a dark haired girl about 26, and Josey a blonde, aggressive South African girl. No surprises there. Izzie and I have not discussed any kind exclusivity but I'm getting the impression that she'd quite like it. I feel kind of obliged to take her home I think she'd be quite pissed at me if I didn't, but I really want to fuck Josey. Mostly because up until now she's only given me a hand-job and let me finger her and get her tits out. Man! Her tits are, I have to admit, some of the best fun bags I've ever encountered. I get a hard on just thinking about them. TITS!!!! FUCKING TITS!!! TITS!!! TITTTSS!!!! TIIIITTTTTTTSSSSS!! FUCKING, FUCKING FUCKING FUCKING TITTY TIT TITS!! Goddamn it, TITS are the best thing since sliced bread!!

(yeah, but that's just an idiom!

You're an idiot!

No, I said idiom.

You're an idiot!

No…. you're an idiot for not knowing what an idiom is!) I'm slightly paraphrasing Alan Partridge here!

Josey only really fancies me because I'm different to what she is used to. She currently has a boyfriend (soon to be husband no doubt) that she's been with for about 5 years who works in banking or some shite and I suppose I represent the bad and dirty side of her that she's never been able to indulge in, and it excites her but she won't fuck me because she feels guilty, but I'm still taking her home. I do feel a bit bad though because my mate Greg that works with her clearly fancies her but, with no disrespect to the guy, he hasn't got a hope in hell. He's a lovely fella but unfortunately, he hasn't been gifted with good looks. Life is shit that way. It is a real shame that it's often this way but then do our looks shape our personality? Though, then again, he's a nice chap who's not all that attractive and he fancies a girl who is attractive but has a terrible personality. It's an attraction based purely on aesthetics. He's kind of playing himself at

his own game. I do it too, of course. I wish
to the Andromeda galaxy and back I didn't. I
want to date someone with some goddamned
integrity for once in my life. I wish I had
some more goddamned integrity myself.
I jump down from my dancing spot on the
table and I'm feeling pretty drunk. You tend
to get drunk pretty quick after being on
stage. It's the adrenaline and blood pumping
around your body at 100 miles per hour
firing the alcohol straight into your brain
box. It's ace. I head into the toilets. The
toilets as in most pubs in Camden are a shit
hole, literally and metaphorically. I go
into the cubicle, preferring some privacy
and some bastard's left a nugget stewing in
the bottom of the bowl like a tea bag in the
bottom of a mug of cold water. It's looking
right at me and it's putting me right off my
piss. If it winks, I'm out of here. I'm
trying not to disturb it with my piss so it
doesn't start releasing any poo spores out
and up into my nostrils and thus poisoning
my lungs and brain causing a poo tree to
grow out of my hearing ears.
I head back into the bar and everyone is
still partying but the numbers are starting
to dwindle and soon enough they're ringing
the bell for last orders. As often is the
case, post a gig we go on to party at one of
our places depending on the location of the
venue. So I announce to the remaining 15 or
so people that we're heading back to mine to
carry on. Everyone's up for it! The beauty
of this plan is also that I can take all the
potential women back to mine and if one or
two pass out or leave I still have options
however, as previously mentioned, it can
create a bit of tense atmosphere at times.
There is one problem. Trying to herd 10 to
20 drunk people from one part of the town to

the other can be a logistical nightmare and
you inevitably end up loosing a few due to
drunkenness, tiredness or getting lost-ness.
We manage to grab a load of black cabs out
on the street and bundle into the back seat
falling over our guitar cases and other band
paraphernalia. We play a spot of 'Topshop'
in the back of the cab, which we picked up
from the Mighty Boosh.

'Johnny if you pulled your own leg off and
planted it on an uninhabited island do you
think you could grow more legs and become
the king of the leg people?' I inquire.
'Well. I'm glad you asked me that. It has
been playing on my mind for some time.'
Replied Johnny. 'As it happens I already
have put this plan into work and I'm
expecting to observe my first crop of legs
this very spring.' He exclaimed.

'Are you pulling my leg?' Chris says
regretting his error instantly.

Andy points out on all of our behalf that,
'We're not angry with you. We're just
disappointed.'

We all shake our heads at him. That's what
we do to shame each other. We silently shake
our heads with a look of disappointment and
mild contempt.

We all clamber out of the cabs on arrival
and a few of the cabs behind ours arrive
soon after and there's a few bewildered
people waiting at the front entrance to my
flat. We ascend up the stairs and into my
flat and we dig out all the booze we bought
on route at the 24hr off licence. I stick a
record on and we all carry on drinking into
the night. As the night goes on I'm trying
to assess my female situation. Who's
definitely still interested, who's not
interested, and am I too pissed to get it up
anyway. Izzie and Jess help me to make the

decision. Izzie leaves in a bit of strop due to a lack of attention and Jess is sick in the toilet and now sleeping on the sofa. We have at this point all removed our t-shirts and some of the girls have done so too and we're all dancing and singing.

Andy is having a smoke out the window and whilst he's looking outside enjoying his cigarette, I creep up behind him, unzip my fly and then just lay my flaccid penis on the top of his back. Him not realising it's my cock (it's not that big clearly) just says,' Hello mate.'

Until he turns his head slightly to see my willy laying on his back and shoots up like a whippet. Everyone one laughs hysterically and then to my dismay I turn to discover Chris has his cock out too. He's just generally showing it to the world outside so I give it a good old slap, "Ayyyeee,' he squeals, half laughing. After a bit more fun and frivolity I lead Josey into my bedroom. We start to snog whilst still standing with my hands around her waist. I can still hear the music in the living room and the lads messing around. I push her down onto the bed forcefully and I am very keen and impatient to get those two fun bags out into the fresh air. I pull her top over her head and quickly unfasten her bra whilst we continue to kiss. Quite soon we're both naked and I part her legs to slide a finger inside her. She is soaking wet as she always is which has made the not fucking her even more ball-aching. I decide that tonight's the night. After playing with her nipples and her clit for while, wanking her to a climax I climb on top of her. I hold her arms above her and rub my cock on her clit and lips. I push my cock very slowly inside her, gauging if she's going to let this happen. When it's fully inside and I think okay I'm safe it's in, I build up a bit of a slow rhythm and I can see she's breathing heavily with her eyes closed. Then she says, 'Don't! Stop it!'

She keeps saying this but not offering any real resistance, which confuses the fuck out of me. Does she really want me to stop? Am I raping her? It then dawns on me what this situation is. She doesn't want to feel guilty about cheating on her boyfriend and so if she says no and I still fuck her it's not her fault so I continue to fuck her whilst holding both her wrists above her head with just one hand. It does feel a bit like rape because she's still saying no but whilst still breathing and sighing heavily and squirming around in delight. She's so wet and I've wanted to fuck her for quite a while and despite the amount of booze in my body, which usually makes you last for ages I can feel I'm going to cum very soon. Knowing this, I start fucking her faster and harder so I get the full feel of the release when I cum and plus she is a fucking bitch so I want to fuck her like one. It's that kind of teach the little slut a lesson sex. It's a real turn on. I feel sorry for people that go through life only having nice considerate sex. Don't get me wrong it has its place and I have been accused of being too considerate too. As predicted I do quickly cum inside her but she's pretty horny too and has cum a couple times during the act. She lies there for a minute enjoying the afterglow and says 'I told you not to fuck me.'

I just shrug. 'Ah well.'

'I can't stay,' she says.

'Good,' I reply.

She gets up to get dressed and I see my cum trickling out of her pussy and down the inside of her leg. 94.
I head back into the lounge where the party's died down a bit and everyone's seated having a drink a smoke and a chat. I pour myself a Sailor Jerry's and coke with ice and a slice of lime. I collapse onto the sofa and enjoy a rollie whilst listening to 'She's so heavy' by the Beatles turned up loud and I look across at the lads and think. I love my boys, my boys (Monty!…You terrible cunt!).

x Boxes x

Luckily I have a bit of cash saved up in the old bank box and, before I quit my job at Stream Creek, I had already booked a trip to Thailand. I know what you're thinking. I didn't book Thailand because I wanted to go on a sex holiday. Or did I subconsciously? I think that genuinely isn't the purpose of my trip but having said that, every person I've told that I'm going there, come to think of it, did give me a knowing look. It made me feel a bit dirty and slightly ashamed of myself. And then I think, 'Fuck it.' I don't care. That is the kind person I am. Or am I? Yes, I think I am. If I had more money I know I would fuck more prostitutes. They are wonderful. You just fuck them and then leave. What's not to like? It's only because I'm tight and I've done okay getting laid in normal life that I haven't slept with more of them. I still think that having sex with the general public is a great deal better, no doubt but I suppose it's the seediness of screwing a prostitute that's exciting.
One of the downsides of being perpetually single of course is that you've not got anyone to go on holiday with. By my age, most of your mates are pretty much all hooked up with a girlfriend. Luckily, Thailand is just the place to travel to if you're on your tod. There's plenty of backpackers milling around who need company and lots of couples who are desperate to talk to someone, anyone but the person they came on holiday with. I avoid those types. There's no one to shag in that situation and they're usually quite boring. That's the problem with holidays. You get a loving

couple that are usually busy doing their shit jobs and watching Hollyoaks omnibuses and then when they go on holiday and all they've got for entertainment is each other and they realise that they've got nothing to say to each other. That's what terrifies me. I don't mind sitting in silence with someone that you're connected with. Sometimes I prefer it. It's good to know when to shut your mouth hole and just sit peacefully and enjoy the moment.

I've got 10 days booked in Thailand and a fair few miles to cover. I land in Bangkok early in the morning, it's a massive airport full of tourists and businessmen and I can't help looking around trying to decipher who is here on a sex holiday. I get a train from the airport to save cash. I probably should just get a taxi. I get off the train and have not got the faintest idea how to find the hostel I'm staying at and it's boiling hot and I'm lugging everything around in a heavy backpack. I know I've packed too much as we all do. Apparently they say when you travel, before you leave you're supposed to just empty half your suitcase out and take what's left. That's all you need supposedly. Well, that's fine but what if you empty the half with all your toiletries, clothes, and passport in and the half you end up taking is an inflatable lilo that happens to take up the other half of your suitcase, you're going to be a bit screwed then aren't you. I hail down a tuk-tuk and give the guy the address and we zip off. We turn up at my hostel in a fairly busy part of the backpacking district. I like the feel of the place. I get myself up to my room after checking in. It's very basic but who cares, I'm just sleeping here. It's almost a bit depressing which does make you want get the

hell out of there. I stick some shorts on. I hate me in shorts. My legs are too thin and white. I look okay until I put some footwear on. I don't know why this is. I look okay in barefoot or maybe flip-flops though no British milky white guy can really pull those off either. I look fairly ridiculous in everything else. I am capable of getting a tan but it's been so long since I was in the sun for any length of time that my skin takes forever to absorb it. Mostly, other people get brown off my reflection. I put a vest on, grab my effects, and head out into the hot sticky streets. I decided I want to get a bit of culture while I'm here before I do my usual trick of drinking too much, staying up until the wee hours and not wanting to get up the next/same day.
I grab a map from the hostel reception and take a seat outside and enjoy a dark rum and coke and a rollie. Usually I don't like to smoke in the heat for some unknown reason. It's okay though, I have a parasol shading me from the sun. I have a gander at the map and make a rough plot of the temples around the city. I start to make my way to the first temple and I decide that I'll do the tour of the temples on foot. I often like to walk to places rather use public transport however I then usually soon realise that the destination is much further than I had anticipated and then I find I'm hot, lost and frustrated. I'm not sure that my sense of direction is as attuned as I'd like to imagine it is. 45 minutes later I arrive at the first temple with a giant 80ft golden Buddha inside. The temple is charming enough but it also seems quite tacky like a dilapidated fat gold fella theme park. The paint is falling off the walls and the giant Buddha looks like a cheap film prop. I do

that thing people do at art galleries where you walk around trying to feel something spiritual or look pensively at something on the wall when other people are around when secretly you're thinking, 'This is shit!' It's like when people are at an art gallery show that they don't really understand or like what they see and they're pretending that they do. The most stupid of all art-appreciating wankers are the ones who actually convince themselves that what they are observing is in fact brilliant and why they spend so much money on bullshit art so they don't feel like such a cunt. Although I don't know how they justify it to themselves standing there saying, 'Oh darling, oh darling, it's so, so mystifying and magical. The artist must have really suffered to create such a piece!', when a security guard points out that it's just a Glade air freshener that someone left in the plug socket. I leave quite soon and walk to the next temple. This temple is much smaller and the architecture is very beautiful and the temple inside is very calm and very cool and very relaxing. I sit inside the cool of the stone/marble temple and gaze upon the flowers, candles, burning incense sticks and various sculptures. I don't feel reflective in any sense but it is relaxing. I stay for 20 minutes inhaling the incense and step out into the heat and on to the next temple, noticing on my exit that right behind the temple is a an iMax cinema, which somewhat ruins the serenity of the moment. It takes me about another 40 minutes to get to the next temple and I'm becoming a little irritable at the heat and effort I'm exerting. Why don't I just get in tuk—tuk? On route to Wat Saket, I stop by a little local shaded street food restaurant next to the river. I order some noodles and a fruit juice drink mixed with what I think is tea. I've no idea what it is exactly but it tastes pretty good and it's cold and refreshing. I see a white western woman enter the restaurant and I have an aching feeling to talk to her. I don't mind being on my own but sometimes when you're in a very foreign country and you don't know anyone and you haven't really got a clue what you're going to do with yourself, a bit of conversational familiarity is most welcome. Also it helps that she is a woman. I bet if it was a bloke I wouldn't be anywhere near as interested in holding a conversation with them. Well maybe, depending on the guy. I'd rather be on my own than have a shit conversation with some random fella, even though I seem quite happy to entertain relatively dull conversations with women with very little to say. Not for that long though to be fair. If we get to the point of having sex then I'll probably move on quite quickly. Once you've slept with someone they often lose attraction to you. It's a bit like the Wizard of Oz. At first he is a large, mysterious, intriguing and wondrous thing that is insurmountable, and then you peer behind the curtain and it's nothing more than a small frail old man.

I think about approaching her but she looks perfectly engrossed in whatever is happening in her own head. She looks like an intelligent, focused and hard-working woman with virtue. She is a little intimidating in some ways. She is the kind of woman I'd like to spend more time with but she would probably see straight through me and into my dark hollow soul and be completely disinterested in me and rightly so. I bottle it, and make my excuses as to why there's no point in my talking to her. 5 minutes later a man of equal intelligence and virtue arrives and gives her a kiss. Bastard! That's a kick in gut. Ah well. They look right for each other and they look happy too, so good for them. I finish my refreshments and walk back out onto the street.

I arrive at the temple 30 minutes later. It's the highest temple in Bangkok I believe or at least one of them. I think the Western name for it is Golden Mount. It has a spiralling path up the side of the building that is made from cobbled stones. Half way up the pathway you come to a selection of large bells you can give a good clanging to and there's also a giant bell that's larger than a rhino. I give it a good old wallop with a log attached to a chain swing. I ascend to the top of the temple where there is a 360-degree view of the city. Inside the temple there are people lighting incense sticks and sticking them next to a golden Buddha laying down in a sort of porn/paint me pose.

I take some time to absorb the view above Bangkok. I think I've seen enough temples for one day and start to make my way back to the hostel. On route I come across a 90-metre road that has been abandoned by all life with around 15 or so cars turned over or burnt out like a scene from some sort of an apocalyptic zombie movie. It's very eerie. There have been many political protests lately regarding the peoples' opposition to their government. I get back to the hostel and take a shower and get dressed and ready for the evening, which involves more or less what I've been wearing

all day. Even in the evening it's too hot to wear more than shorts and a vest.
I go out onto the busy bustling street that's filled with market traders selling food and random tat that nobody needs, such as bracelets with your name sewn into them, laser pens, lighters. Actually I do need one of these items. The bastards at the airport took my lighter assuming that I wanted to burn the plane down. I find a local place to eat, I'm pretty hungry from all that walking. I get some sort of local noodle and chicken dish and a local branded bottle of beer. I sit and roll a cigarette, lean back in a wicker chair, sip my beer and watch the people passing by. The street is filled with tourists, backpackers and a few old Western men with their Thai girlfriends. Poor fuckers. The strange thing is that the Thai women they have selected aren't even very attractive. Surely if you're going to give up cognitive, intellectual conversation with someone you actually have something in common with, for someone you just want to fuck, surely you want to make sure they are damned hot. I finish my food and neck my beer and walk into the heart of the street. I'm eyeing up the various bars trying to decide which one to try first. Naturally I'm looking for ones with women in. When you're on your own and looking for someone to talk to it makes you feel like it's your first day at school and you feel quite exposed and like a bit of an idiot. Feeling a bit foolish standing around trying to pick which place to go into, I end up panic-picking one. It's the wrong one. I take a seat outside at a white plastic table as it's still around 28 degrees and someone comes and takes my order. I order a beer and roll another cigarette. I look around and there's

not much going on in this bar and I can just
see beyond the heavily pedestrianised
street, the bar where I clearly should have
gone. A couple next to me are sitting with
each other and as often is the case they
have fuck all to say to each other. They
clock me sitting alone and I can sense that
they are desperate to talk to someone else,
anybody else but the person they came on
holiday with.
'Hi. Are you from England?' The fat, be-
speckled boyfriend says.
'Yeah,' I reply disinterestedly. Trying not
to be too rude but not too inviting either.
'Whereabouts?' She asks.
'London,' I reply.
The conversation continues in this way for
about 10 minutes, which is the time it takes
me to drink my beer and get the hell away
from them.
'Well. Nice to meet you.' I say
'Bye!' They say in stereo looking like
abandoned puppies being left in the house
that don't understand why you're leaving and
are you ever coming back.
The nice-to-meet-you statement must have
quickly seemed like a lie as they must have
watched me cross over the street and sit
outside the bar opposite in pursuit of more
interesting or sexier people.
I'm sitting alone once again in the new
livelier, hipper bar. About 15 minutes later
an English good-looking lad in his twenties
with a shaved head and a well earned tan
comes up to me and says
'Hey mate, do you want to join us?'
'Thanks, yeah, that would be good.'
I go and join him and his mate. They're both
quite laddish and not really my kind of
people however I really appreciated the
gesture. It was kind of him to ask me. They

are both browned seasoned veterans of the area having worked a summer here in bars. Another big German guy they befriended earlier also joins us and we play a drinking game called 'Skoosh'. I start to get pretty pissed after an hour of this drinking game. They announce a few girls are coming to join us soon and I perk up a bit on hearing this. 'Try and guess which one I'm banging,' the more idiotic and misogynistic of the two blurts out. It might be fair to say that my attitude to women may not always seem, well, far from perfect but I don't think any less of women or that they are below men and I certainly would not talk about the woman I'm 'banging' in such a public and derogatory manner. I treat all people equally which is admittedly with a level of disdain but I do just really fancy women and want to have sex with lots of them. Is that derogatory? This statement puts me right off this guy, and I wasn't that keen on him to begin with. When the girls turn up, the girl he's 'banging' is actually quite attractive and is, in fact, excited to see the massive ape-brained twat. It annoys the shit out of me. There are three girls and one of them is quite rotund and unattractive and the other one is dark-haired and slim and definitely someone I'd like to have sex with. All of the girls are fairly tanned and they look and unsurprisingly talk like chavs. I detest chavs but I'm still hypocritical enough to have sex with them. I had sex with a 44-year-old chav mother from Essex earlier in the year. I met her on a dating site. The very same day she was sending me photos of her massive tits and sending me videos of her fucking herself with a dildo. Dirty bitch. We had phone sex and both wanked ourselves off. That weekend I went over to

her house. She picked me up from the train
station in her bright white BMW and drove me
back to hers. Her kids were with their dad,
thank god. Inside the house it was a typical
hairdresser's style décor. Expensive and
tacky. There was a white leather sofa for
god's sake. She opened a pair of Peronis and
we sat on the sofa and she put shit Saturday
night TV on. She had short bleached blonde
hair and looked good for her age and I
couldn't wait to get my hands around her
massive tits. Within about 5 minutes we got
straight down to some full-mouthed kissing
and I removed her clothes sharpish. I pulled
her jeans down and she's wearing a black
skimpy thong. No surprises there. She lies
down on the fake fur rug that's on the sofa.
It's very comfortable for fucking on. She
has one of those terrible L-shaped sofas
although they are very useful for sex. I
pull her knickers down, climb on top her and
we have a really good, hard, enthusiastic
screw, and her tits did not disappoint.
Fucking massive they were. We fuck a couple
more times over the duration of the evening,
and then again in her bed. Both knowing that
there's a good chance we won't see each
other again, we make sure we have sex again
in the morning. In her Essex accent she
says, 'I needa put sum lube on me fanny,
babe. It's a bit sore from all the sex, ya
know.'

She applies a hand full of sloppy lube and
gets on top of me and starts to fuck me. She
says it hurts and can I get on top instead.
I take it gentle with her and I can tell
it's still hurting her, which turns me on
even more and no in no time we're both
cumming in spite of her discomfort. She
drops me off at the train station, gives me

a kiss on the lips and I say my goodbyes. I never contact her again or she me.

The three girls sit down and the moron's girl is on his lap with her arms wrapped around him. I try to make small talk with the more attractive of the other two but I'm not getting much back from her and she seems disinterested or playing hard to get. I'm really not sure about the situation and I'm quite drunk now and I'm terrible at small talk at the best of times. They're all chatting away and I can feel I'm fading from the group so I get up and go to toilet, plus I can feel I need a shit which I'm dreading. Thai toilets are fairly grim. One thing I struggle with is squatting when I'm trying to do a poo. I just have to sit down but looking at the toilet seat, there's no fucking way I'm sitting on that. I deposit my insides whilst supporting my weight in a squat position and soon I feel much better. It's rather late now but it's still swelteringly hot. A sweaty poo isn't the most fun I've ever had. Quite quickly to my dismay I notice there is no toilet roll. Shit! I look around in desperation for a solution. My solution comes in the form of a 'bum gun'. A bum gun is essentially a hosepipe with a trigger, of which I have never encountered before. I give the trigger a quick blast and fire it at the toilet door by mistake. It's fucking powerful. It's more like a jet wash than a hosepipe. Right. Lets give this a go then. I lift my bottom up and aim the gun. The first shot hits me in the left cheek. I re aim and it fires quite powerfully right up my bum hole. It's actually quite enjoyable. I give it a good blasting, though you become aware you're not sure what happens to all the shrapnel. Some of it must be spraying back onto the hose that I'm holding and onto the walls. By the time I'm done the lower half of my body is pretty soaked and so is the toilet cubicle. The only problem now, is there no way to dry myself, so now I have a soaking wet arsehole and bottom with water dripping down my legs. With it being so damn hot it actually quickly dries up to a reasonable level and I put my shorts back on and also it's a dimly lit bar. I have to say that it does seem a much better system than bog roll, despite the initial disaster, and it does feel a great deal cleaner. Better than a dry wipe methinks, and better for the environment, I presume.

I go up to the bar and order a dark rum and coke and I see there's a girl sitting on her own at the bar. She has a cracking figure and looks pretty damn hot. I start to talk to her and I'm coming up with some fairly creative chat, to say I'm half cut, and she seems to be receptive to it and is keen to talk to me, so I take a seat next to her and do my best to hold a decent conversation. We talk until closing time and out on the street she makes it clear that she is going home alone and not with me but she gives me a goodbye snog. During our conversation she revealed that she is staying at the same island as me, Kho Phi Phi, in a few days and we agree to meet there. When she leaves I feel a bit despondent and don't really feel like going home but all the bars are closing and it's 2am. I walk along the abandoned street and I stumble across a group of people congregated around someone playing the guitar. I sheepishly take a pew and some lady selling beers comes over.

I spy a couple of girls standing and chatting and watching. One of the girls has long dark brown hair and looks to be about 22. She's really attractive and very cool-looking, like one of those chicks in American high school movies that's well out of your league so you just gawp at them rather than actually speak to them. I can see that the trendy guy talking to them is trying his luck with her so I avert my attention back to the music. The guy playing holds out the guitar to ask if anyone wants to play it and there are no takers so I say I'll have a go. I'm a little apprehensive as I'm not exactly sure how drunk I am at this point. Luckily my fingers seem to work fine and my voice also seems to be in good form. I play one of my own songs and get a round of applause and the hot girl has also taken a seat next to me and offers me some of her cocktail she's made in a plastic bottle. I play another song and offer the guitar back to the guy. I don't want to. I want to keep playing it but you don't want to seem like you're a show-off, even though that's exactly what I am. Fortunately the guy says, 'Play again man. I've run out of songs anyway.'

I apologise to the group and tell them that I don't really know many covers but I can play some more of my own stuff and they seem okay with it. I play a couple more songs and everyone's getting into it and they are in good spirits. I hand the guitar back and chat to the hot American girl, Amy, I discover her name is. After half an hour the group begins to disband and people disappear into the early morning light like mist. Amy asks if I want to come with her and her friend. She appears to have ditched the other guy. I don't know where we're going and I don't question it either. I just follow them through the dirty alleyways filled with empty plastic bottles, newspapers, and the general crap people leave behind after a night out. We are animals us human beings with no respect for our planet or those around us. I don't drop litter, it's just plain inconsiderate and rude. I've no idea what's happening really, or what her intention is, but I'm excited and uncertain at the same time.

We end up at the apartment she's renting. It's very basic, just as mine is. The bad news is she has no booze although I've probably had enough. 'I'll go and get us some booze. I'll be back in a minute,' I say.

I head outside and I buy a pack of beers and a large bottle of clean drinking water. There is none to speak of in her room and you don't want be drinking out of taps unless you're starting to become fond of those bum-guns. I go back up to her room and knock on the door. There's no answer. I knock again and still no answer. I'm stood there in the hall without a clue what the hell is going on. I'm a bit drunk and beginning to question if I've got the right room or even the right floor. Shit! She doesn't have my number and I don't have hers and I'm thinking I'm fucked now and I don't know where the hell I am either. I get a chance to get with a girl I really fancy and I manage to lose her or worse, she's run away.

I trust that I have the right room and go down to reception, if you can call it that and ask to borrow the spare key as I have locked myself out. Luckily the guy has no idea who is staying in his hotel and who is not, otherwise I'd never have been given a key. It's a bit frightening really. I go back up to the room and put the key in the

door, still not quite sure what to expect. The door opens and I see Amy asleep on the bed. Fuck. I was only gone 5 minutes and she was the one who invited *me* back.
'Hey!' I say and she stirs.
'Sorry, I fell asleep.'
I hand her a beer and I open one for myself. I sit next to her and we chat for a bit about our careers, travel and religion, which is usually a bad idea. She's an intelligent and interesting girl. She's 23 and has been travelling the world for about 6 months.
She kisses me and informs me we won't be having sex. We go to sleep around 7am and at some point in the midst of drifting in and out of sleep we do have sex. Why do women say that so often, that we won't be having sex and then they do? She has a nicely toned and tanned body and it's a nice lazy fuck. 95. Unfortunately she has to be up at 8am and so I have to leave with about one hour's sleep. When I awake I feel absolutely destroyed. I somehow find my way back to my hostel and collapse onto the bed and I don't awake until it's dark again. This is always quite disorientating and makes you a bit angry at yourself for wasting an entire day, however I think I earned it. It was pretty much a perfect first night.

One day later I catch a flight to Krabi. From there I take a bus and then have to get a boat to West Railay beach. Unbeknownst to some of my fellow holidaymakers, the boat that takes us to the destination does not dock at a port so you have to walk out into the sea well above your waist. Luckily I have a backpack but some of these unlucky folks have massive suitcases, but they do have wheels, which really helps on the sea

floor. Poor planning. Luckily for them, the boatman is reluctantly on hand. The vehicle is an old Long-tail boat with what looks and sounds like a diesel car engine just dumped on the back of it and somewhat ruining the serenity of the Thai beach. We clamber on board, take our pews and off we go.
30 minutes later we approach the beach and it really is idyllic and beautiful with the odd, alien-like massive rock islands poking out of the sea as though they fell from outer space. We depart the boat, again in the sea, and carry our luggage onto dry land. It hurts your feet once you reach the rocky part of the beach and I'm regretting not bringing some more suitable footwear. There is forestry all around the sandy beach and lots of little charming bars hidden within this shaded paradise. My accommodation is a wooden shack with no air conditioning but good clean showers. I like it here. I venture down to the beach and look for a good spot. Preferably near some normal or sexy looking people. I see a few fitting that description and pitch up close to them but not weirdly close. Quite soon after pitching a lady approaches me. She's Swedish I think and she asks me for a light and I think, this is a good start. I however can think of nothing interesting or witty to say in the moment and before I know it she's handing me back my lighter.
'Thanks.'
'No problem.'
And she's gone. Damn!
After sitting in the sweltering heat for 15 minutes I'm already slightly agitated and fidgety so I head to the beach bar and buy a couple of beers. I settle back down onto the beach and look at the horizon and watch people swimming and playing in the sea.

There's a few couples playing bat and ball games and kissing and looking generally in love and it makes me envious and I feel quite lonely all of a sudden. I shake it off and try to remember where I am and how fortunate I am to be here.
After a couple of beers and a rollie I pop into the sea feeling a little light-headed. I need to cool down and take a surreptitious piss. I'm trying to relieve myself without looking like I am so I try swimming at the same time but it's quite difficult to swim and piss at the same time so I stand and look around as if I'm just enjoying the scenery trying not to pull a strained, concentrating type face. I wonder if I pissed on a fish (Jelly fish!!!).
I return to my towel and dry off and pick up my book and read for a couple of hours. I spy a pale white girl with medium-length white hair who looks quite bohemian and mildly insane. She seems to be sort of floating/dancing around the beach. She looks to be happy with her own company or perhaps she's just pretending to be, as she also looks as though she wouldn't mind some human contact. She floats closer to me and I catch her eye and say, 'Hi'.
'Hi'. She says. 'Where are you from?'
'London'. I reply.
'Oh cool'. She says.
'Where are you from?' I enquire.
'Romania. I'm Anja' she says.
'Blake.' I reply.
As she has virtually ice white hair it's hard to tell, but I'm fairly certain she has unshaven armpits but has at least shaved her legs, or I can't see that either. When she points at something I see that, yes, she does have hairy armpits and I nearly vomit in my own mouth. I know it's ridiculous to

have such an aversion to hair on women but I
really do. I just don't like a woman to be
hairier than me, but I don't mind that downy
type blonde hair. To be fair, I am the most
hairless man I know. Not a follicle to be
found on my chest or butt cheeks. I think
it's because I have a full head of hair with
no current sign of it receding. My granddad
died with a full head of hair at 84, as did
my dad at 66. I've noticed that most balding
men have very hairy chests. Perhaps it's one
or the other, a bit like a piece of string.
When the hair starts to sink into their
heads and out of their chest they could just
pull it back up. Sorted. Or use a thousand
mini clamps or so to stop the descent. I
really don't like hairy fannies as oral sex
is not fun. It's like pleasuring a small
mammal and, as I discovered when I was 17
with my first sexual partner, you cannot
swallow pubes. I do like a *bit* of hair
however. A strip. A fully nude minge makes
you feel like a paedophile and it can make a
vagina look like a newly born chick with a
rash.
Anja seems interesting or good at pretending
to be. She's been travelling for about 9
months and tells me she has not found
anywhere to stay yet on this beach. I'm not
sure if she's angling for a place to stay
seeing as we've only just met. It's a risky
question but I think fuck it, I'll risk it.
'Do you want to stay at mine?'
'Yeah, that'd be cool, man. Thanks.'
I can't tell if she is just a complete
freeloader or if sex is on cards. In the
activity of talking we fail to notice that
the tide is drawing in at an alarming rate
and the path to the other side of the beach
where I am staying has been cut off. It's
also getting dark. We consider climbing the

rocks across but decide against it. We head
back to where we were and there is one
remaining taxi boat about to depart to our
side of the island. We jump on the boat
along with 3 Australians. There are two lads
and a woman. It's a bit dark but the Ozzie
gal looks quite attractive but a bit chubby
I think. The Ozzie woman and I seem to form
an instant rapport. I say something slightly
amusing about our predicament and she laughs
and retorts, taking the piss out of me. I
like her spirit, but I can't tell if she's
with one of the lads as they're not saying
anything. It's pretty dark when we get off
the boat and as we exit, the Ozzie invites
us to join them for dinner, as it's her
birthday, to which I agree.
Anja and I head back to my apartment and we
both take a shower, not together. We head
out and after walking through the forest for
10 minutes we come upon the restaurant
they're seated at.
'Hi!' I say
'Hey!' they reply.
We sit down and I notice the woman is older
than I thought she was but has a sort of
muscular build and nice shoulders and arms
and a dark tan and long dark hair to her
shoulders. I like a bit of muscle on a lady.
The two lads look pretty young and I can't
quite figure out the dynamic.
'I'm Tara and this is my son Aaron and his
mate Paul. They've never been outside of Oz
before so I thought I'd take them away.'
So all is now clear. She is a very
attractive older woman. I later discover she
is 40, and looks damn good for it too.
'How do you two know each other?' Tara says,
which makes me think she's fishing for info,
which could mean she's interested but
there's no clear indication.

'We just met 1 hour before we met you,' I say.
We make idle chit-chat for a bit and Anja is becoming a bit irritating, voicing strong opinions that don't really mean anything. It's clear she's a bit of a bullshit hippy. Anja says, 'it's stupid to ask someone what they do for a living as it doesn't sum them up.'
I say, 'it may not sum them up but it still tells you quite a lot about them.'
She babbles on about some other hippy bollocks ideas that no one else is taking seriously.
It turns out Tara is an aerialist which explains her physique.
The two lads, it's clear, have never left probably their own town. They are quite simple boys and very boring. The son seems intelligent enough but has zero charisma. We order our food and down a few local Thai beers. I'm feeling a bit tipsy now. After dinner we go to a little rustic outdoors bar, accompanied by the sound of the waves and the tickle of a mellifluous light breeze flowing through the warm coastal air.
We shoot a few games of pool. Tara and I team up to play doubles and we are getting noticeably closer to each other and standing so close to each other we're touching. I have lost all interest in Anja and she is lying out on the cushions spread in a little elevated section of the bar. The lads are drinking soft drinks. Anja says she's tired and can sense there's something going on and says she's going to head back to the shack but that she'll sleep outside on the bench. It's certainly warm enough and I don't object. Tara and I have a couple of rum and colas and we're getting quite merry. The lads want to leave but it's only about

11.30pm. She says she should go but I tell her it's her birthday and she should celebrate. She goes off to tell her son and Paul that she's staying out. As they go to leave, her son sort of gives me a look like, 'You're going to fuck my mum aren't you!' I look back him signalling that yes, I probably will.

They both sod off and we head to another bar. We take a couple of stools at a little beach bar, order two more rums and two shots of gold tequila. She downs it and is looking all of a sudden quite pissed. There's a couple of mid-twenties lads also at the bar which seem to be drawing her drunk attention and I start think I'm losing her or maybe I'm just being paranoid. She soon draws her attention back to me and announces she's pissed and needs to be sick. We head onto the beach and sit on the sand and she throws up. I've brought us a couple of beers so she swills that down and seems to be back to relative normality. We start to kiss and very quickly we're all over each other. I lay on top of her and she's tells me to fuck her. It's pitch black other than the light from the full moon. I can see there are a couple of girls walking around the beach. I don't know if they can see us and quite frankly I don't give a damn. I pull her knickers to the side and slide my cock inside her. Usually when I'm this drunk I can't cum but her drunkenness has sobered me a little and fucking on the beach is turning me on big time. I'm fucking her and it's fucking incredible. A perfect holiday fuck scenario. I tell her I'm going to cum and she tells me to cum in her mouth. I pull my cock out of her pussy, move my body up and put my cock in her mouth. I pump her mouth a couple of times and before I know it I'm cumming hard in her mouth and she moans with pleasure. It's fucking amazing when a girl takes you in her mouth after you've been inside her and you cum all over her tonsils. Fuck it feels fucking brilliant. Fucking wonderful ball emptying fulfilment. I feel so happy and content. We sit on the beach, and she sits in between my legs facing away from me seeming equally content. I roll a smoke and enjoy the rest of my beer. We head back to my place and Anja is fast asleep on the bench. Silly cow.

In the morning Tara and I fuck again and once again when I'm about to cum she tells me to cum in her mouth and I happily do. She takes it hungrily and moans and groans with satisfaction. What a godsend. We head off into the warm morning sun together and we say our goodbyes. 96.

x It's the final countdown x

So, The Winter Kicks have made it to the final of the bullshit battle of the bands competition. After 3 gruelling rounds of annoying the fuck out of our friends to come and see us play, buy tickets and vote for us, we've at last got to the final.
The final is being held at the HMV Forum in Kentish Town, which for a small-time band such as us is fucking massive. The inside of the venue looks like a grand beautiful old twenties theatre. Adorned with gold painted ornate banisters and royal red carpets and grand light fixtures. We can't quite believe it. It's even more spectacular when it's completely empty. You can feel the ghosts of past performances lingering in the air as you inhale their history with a sense of lachrymose, hope and wonder. My boys, my boys!
We're all buzzing with excitement, as we get set up for sound check. The stage feels massive and makes me feel quite small. To kill time we go and grab a pint but we're tempering ourselves and agreed not to get pissed beforehand. The wait before the performance feels like someone's removed the batteries from the clock. Some of our friends arrive, and my beautiful sister Paula and my brother-in-law Marcus, too. I love my sister very much. She's one of the funniest, considerate and driven people I know. She does have a bit of temper every now and then, which is something she inherited from my father unfortunately. Luckily for her she married a man that has the patience of a saint who just laughs at her if she's being ridiculous and the

situation is diffused. If she and I were married, which I think is not only weird but also illegal, we would last about 10 seconds as we'd never back down in an argument. Luckily our platonic sibling relationship does work.
'Hello, Zippy.' my sister says.
When we were kids she always called me Zippy. Perhaps it was because of my anarchic behaviour as a toddler. I used to call her Paw Paw before I had the ability to pronounce her name (Paula) properly.
'Hi, sis.' I say and I give her a proper cuddle and pick her up off the ground and spin her around and she smiles from ear to ear. She has beautifully prominent round cheekbones that accentuate her beaming and genuine child-like smile.
John and Julia are here as always. Always on top form, ready to party and get involved in our ridiculous behaviour. Some of my old flat mates are here also. One thing I have learnt from never learning from my mistakes is that you should never fuck the people you live with, unless they're your wife or girlfriend. Every time you have sex with someone you live with it always, always goes to shit. Especially when you start bringing other girls back to the house and the girl is a real screamer. You can't really tell a girl in the mid-throes of passion to, 'Keep it down a bit'. That was back when I almost had what you might even call a relationship. She was called Mary. We met on a dating site and straight away I could see what a beautiful and genuine person she was. She dressed in a 50s attire and wore her bum-length hair in a sort of beehive. Occasionally she wore it down and she looked incredibly beautiful. She was, I think it would be fair to say, full-figured and had

quite a large bottom that black men on the street seem to think is appropriate to publicly acknowledge. I normally wouldn't go for big bottoms but I really liked hers and when we had sex doggy-style I liked to look at it whilst we were fucking and it really turned me on. Being the fuckwit that I am, I felt she didn't quite tick all my boxes in some sort of an aesthetic way and I found I had a wondering eye and so I ended our relationship. 3 times. I regret this terribly and I know if I was still with her today I would be a better, happier and less misanthropic man. She is a testament to all that's good in the world and I'm a fucking moron. Being in her company was effortless and I don't remember many other occasions in my life that I've laughed so much and felt unadulterated happiness. I think I loved Mary, though it may not have seemed that way.

Fortunately, the band and I have a truly wonderful group of friends and family around us. It's a very special part of our lives and I feel very lucky to be a part of their lives and feel loved. It's a group that has a warm glow of frivolity, rapture and caring all around it. A few old workmates turn up and Johnny, having since been back home turns up 2 hours later with a busload of friends and family from out of town.
The initial band finalist introductions are made by the compere. I don't like waiting to go on stage I always just want to get on with it. After waiting for a certain amount of time I just get a bit angry and so my nerves dissipate into annoyance. Finally, after about 40 minutes of listening to the other bands play, we're on.

'Good luck lads,' I say, and we all give each other a hug.
We walk on stage and the crowd are clapping and whooping and whistling. It's the first time I think I've ever felt like a rock star. I love it. I know it's pathetic to love so much attention but it's terribly addictive. Why do you think people, mostly women, like getting married? Often it's the only time in their life where they are the centre of attention and a star for the day, with people clapping, and whooping, and crying, and all just for you. It's almost to much of a peak into marriage because by the next week you're just back to being the normal you like when the cameras stop rolling in a film and it's not quite as glamorous as you might have thought.
I pick up my guitar and put it over my head and rest the strap across my shoulder. It's a beauty. It's a black and sunburst Custom Fender Telecaster.
'Hello,' I say dryly but with a humoured tone to the crowd.
'We're The Winter Kicks!'
The crowd applauds and calls out in support. We play our first song called Turn Me Black and the energy is electric and we're playing at our very best. We play a couple more songs before slowing the set down slightly to play Lonely Day, which seems to capture the crowd especially as it builds and reaches its crescendo towards the end. We finish the set off with our friends favourite, Lemonade.
By this point our energy is at full throttle and any pre-gig nerves we may have had have long since dissipated and I feel like this is exactly where I'm meant to be. Here up on the stage. I want it so badly it breaks my heart. We smash into the song and the crowd,

or at least the section that know us, sing the word 'Lemonade' back at us when prompted to do so. We get to the end of the song to rapturous applause and I take a bow and we all leave the stage. It's all over in what feels like a heartbeat. We bound off stage like a cluster of electrons in a lighting storm.
'Well done, lads. That was fucking brilliant. My boys, my boys.'
We all give each other a hug.
'Good at singing,' Johnny says.
'Good at drumming,' I reply.
'Good at bass, good at guitar,' we both say to Andy and Chris. There are a few bottles of beers back stage and we chink a good old cheers and neck the bulk of the contents.
We come out from back stage and back into the audience and we're warmly greeted with cheers and congratulations on a great performance from our friends, family and the odd unknown, which is the best compliment, because your mates always say you sound great regardless.
We have drinks waiting for us all, which are gratefully received, and I pretty much down my pint. Thirsty work this singing lark. The problem is I always do down my first and second pint but after coming off stage and after about 3 pints you're feeling fairly merry.
There's only one more band left to play and 25 minutes later it's all wrapped up and the compere comes on stage to inform us that the judges will be making their decision shortly.
'The judges have made their decision as follows'.
'In 4th place is Angle Latitude.
In 3rd place is Vesuvius.
'We're fucked then,' Andy says.

'We also at this point have the awards for best drummer, best guitarist and best vocalist. The winner of best drummer is from the band Smart Alecs.
The winner of the best Guitarist is from The Winter Kicks!'
Everyone cheers. It's brilliant. Chris has bagged himself an award and a two-grand Marshall amp that's fucking massive. We're all so pleased for him but of course hate him for it too because of our terrible envy. Or at least that's how I feel. In his excitement at climbing up onto stage he leaps up and smashes his shin into the stage corner and falls over. What a tit. You can see he's in pain but still smiling from ear to ear as he accepts his award. The problem with this award is that it feels like a consolation prize for not winning the competition so I am now sure that we haven't won.
'The Best vocalist goes to… The Decembers.'
Fuck it, I didn't win. I still think I was the best of the lot. Fucking retards.
'Okay, so back to the main competition. In 2nd place is… Tsunami!!.'
Tsunami are the Japanese band and they were pretty good. I thought they would win it and maybe they should have. I think they didn't win it because how can you have a Japanese winner in the UK competition. The competition is going on worldwide and the winner from each country gets to go and play at a big 3-day music festival in Germany where they compete against each other. It might be a bit strange if the band representing the UK was Japanese.
At this point I'm thinking we're screwed, there's no chance. I've never won a thing in my life. At a village fête I spent so much money trying to win a goldfish the guy felt

sorry for me, so he just gave me the fucking thing. I kept that fish for years, even though they say they die instantly. I was very proud of that. Years later I dug my dad a pond when I was out of work. When they had filled it up I put Skipper my goldfish into the pond in the hope it would grow and enjoy its spacious new surroundings. I later found out that when I left home that he got sucked up one of the pipes because he was too small.

'So, the winner of this year's battle of the bands, with a unanimous decision from the judges, is… The… Winter Kicks!!!!'

'Woooooooaaahhhoooooo, wooooohoo, yeahhhh.' The crowd, or at least our portion of it, cheered rapturously.

We went fucking mental with excitement at having won it. We were pleased as punch and did not celebrate in cool calm rock-n-roll way. We ran onto the stage and we were jumping around like we had a wasp up our trouser leg. We gave each other a good old congratulatory hug and accepted our award with a big fucking smile. Our mates were beaming with joy, too. They had been on the long ride with us and put in their own fair share of hours. This means we're going to be heading to Germany in about a month to compete in the grand international finals. Well done us.

We exit the stage at the back and we are still jumping around like disabled apes. Somehow a Hungarian girl has got back stage and just comes right up to me and says, 'You're the winners aren't you?'

'That's us!' I said.

'I want to suck your dick,' she said in an Eastern European accent.

'Okay'. I reply.

What other response is there. Of course you can suck my dick.
'We're heading to the Purple Turtle in Camden for the after-party, come and join us,' I tell her.
'Okay, I'm coming.'
I'm aware that there are a few lady contenders already in the group but one cannot refuse such an offer, so I'll worry about that later. Right now, my mind is on celebrating and getting smashed.
We head back into the bar of the venue and all our friends are there, cheering and laughing. We get some beers to lubricate ourselves and after sinking 3 tequilas and 3 pints the adrenaline-drunkenness soon kicks in.
We gather up all the troops and head out into the street. We may have just won a competition but we still have to carry our fucking instruments. I bet the Rolling Stones don't have this problem. We grab a few tins from a nearby shop for the journey and flag down a fleet of black cabs. There's about 20 or 30 of us remaining for the after-party. We bundle into the cabs still bubbling with excitement and joy.
We get to the pub in about 10 minutes and head into the venue. It's a pub with regular live bands playing but luckily they've all finished. I think we've all heard enough live music for one night. It's a typical Camden Town pub. It's a bit run down in a nonchalant way. There is paintwork flaking off the walls, the odd poster from yonder years and it smells like a pub should. There's a mild scent of stale beer, cigarette smoke ingrained into the fabric of the building and just enough of a tinge of body odour and muff sweat. We rack up some more drinks, I order a rum and ginger ale,

which is usually a bad idea because I drink them in such haste and don't have the tolerance to match my pace. I need a piss so I head up the creaky wooden stairs. I get to the urinal and the piss flows out without any pushing necessary. I do however push a fart out and in this drunken state I underestimate the strength of my anus and feel a splat of shit against my pants (Americans, we invented English and, yes, pants means underwear). Fuck! This isn't good. This isn't good at all. I have to sort this shit out (excuse the pun) right now. There's only one fucking cubicle and of course it's occupied. I wait for about 5 minutes, which feels like an eternity in poo hell. I'm trying not to move as every time I do I can feel it squishing around. I bang on the cubicle door, 'come on mate.'
The problem with pubs in Camden is that the cubicles are always occupied by people racking up lines of coke which seems to take forever and there's usually two or three of them in there. Lo and behold two people emerge with a devilish & guilty look on their mugs. I slip past them and slam the door shut. I pull down my kegs and it's worse than I thought. These pants are absolutely unsalvageable. I'm going to have to sacrifice my pants to the God of turds. This is a tricky operation because the floor is covered in a layer of sticky god-knows-what and fresh piss and I don't want to drape my jeans in it, or worse, put my socks in it. I remove one leg at a time whilst balancing on my boots. I take my dirty pants off and stuff them behind the toilet. A nice surprise for anyone who looks there! My sincerest apologies to the cleaner. Thank the Lord there is actually toilet roll, which comes as a surprise in a place like

this. I clean myself up until I'm satisfied
all poo traces have been removed. I then
awkwardly put my jeans back on whilst still
balancing on my boots. It always feels weird
putting jeans on when you've got no pants
on. You feel semi naked and a bit vulnerable
like when you've got no shoes on in a crowd.
I leave the cubicle and wash my hands with
just water as there's never any soap and I
head back downstairs.
'You were a long time?' My sister says.
'Oh yeah, I got talking to someone in the
loo,' I reply.
We all have a bit of dance, swilling the
booze around our bellies.
A couple of hours later and it's kicking out
time. 'Back to mine!' I holler.
There are about 10 or so of us left and we
cab it back to mine.
Andy rushes into the loo and later reveals
to me that he also shit his pants and threw
them out of the window onto my neighbour's
flat roof where no doubt some filthy
gluttonous pigeon will feast on them. Back
at the flat there's the band minus Johnny
who had to drive the convoy of his family
and friends back on the bus he hired. Good
lad. There's my sister, Marcus, the South
African gal, Izzie, the Hungarian girl who
wants to suck my dick, John & Julia and a
couple of others. By this point I'm pretty
mushy in the brain department and I can't
quite find the opportunity to latch onto the
Hungarian as I'm too busy arsing around. In
the end I collapse onto the sofa bed my
sister has made up for me and I end up
shagging no one. Bum flaps. In the morning I
discover that the Hungarian ended up
snogging the South African. Makes sense, I
suppose.

A week later the Hungarian and I meet up at my place where I discover she is an erotic dancer and she gives me a demonstration, which is one of the sexiest damn things I've ever seen. Your own private stripper that actually wants to fuck you and isn't pretending to like you! Wonderful! She has the best pair of fake tits. They move around just like normal tits, it took me a while to figure out that they were fake. She is just in her knickers now and then straddles me. She rubs herself against my cock as I'm now miraculously naked myself. She pulls her knickers to the side and slides my cock inside her. One thing is for certain, her dancing has paid off. It's possibly the best fuck I've ever had when the girl's on top. Is there a better sight than a woman with a curvy body, big firm tits riding you like there's no tomorrow. I dare say there isn't. She's doing things that no one has ever done. She also knows how to make herself cum. I don't feel I was doing that much and soon after she does I hastily do the same. I'm very glad that I didn't let that lady get away. 97.

X Where would we would we be without a sense of humour? ....Germany! X

Andy drives us to London City Airport and we're as excited as a paedophile who just found out he inherited Willy Wonka's Chocolate factory. We arrive at the airport and carry our guitars to the check in desk and we're feeling cool as fuck, like we're professional rock stars. We're all trying to keep our cool when secretly we just want to jump up and down and shriek like schoolgirls.
We have a good old giggle on the flight making jokes about the safety guide. One of the warnings seems to be saying 'Beware of black men opening the emergency exit'. We land in Frankfurt around 2pm. We get on a coach that contains all the other bands from around the world and we're all eyeing each up for to see what the competition's like. An hour or so later we arrive at the town where the festival is being held which is called Taubertal. It's a beautiful old town around 2 or 3 hundred years in existence. The festival itself is actually being held in the valley below where all the happy campers are. We fortunately are not camping but staying in a hostel. It's not exactly glamorous but we don't give a shit. The organisers give us a briefing and then we go and dump all our gear off at the room, it's now about 5pm. The sun is still shining and it's pretty hot. It is August after all. We all promised each other that we'd take it easy tonight as we're performing tomorrow. We're here for 3 days but only have to play once. Great!

We find a nice local bar with large wooden benches outside and get ourselves what looks to be a 2 litre glass of beer each. It's bigger than my head.
'Cheers!' Clink, clink, clink.
We order some schnitzels which feels a bit like eating child's food. Simple but tasty! German food generally sucks. We sink a couple of these behemoth beers and I'm already feeling tipsy in this heat. We ask the fella running the place where else is good to go and he points us in yonder direction. He says there's a good bar at the end of town. We walk into the plaza of the town. It's very pretty. We drop into a bar on the square and observe the tourists and other bands and the other festival attendees around us. I'm feeling damn good and relaxed now and not really thinking about tomorrow. We walk out of the square towards the edges of the little town. It's like a fairy tale citadel. It probably was. There is a defensive wall that surrounds the town.
'Arrh, this is it.' I say. 'This the bar that guy mentioned.'
It is a charming dive bar with guitars hanging up on the wall and all the bands had gravitated here and it had a real nice communal feel about it and a group of people were sitting and playing the guitar amongst the punters.
'I like it!' I announced.
We find ourselves a table right in the middle of things and we're drinking some nice cold beers. I'm starting to feel pretty damn merry now. As night falls, we talk to some of the other bands. A Dutch girl group, an Ozzie surfer group, an American group of gimps that think they're cool but look like ABBA if they were a rock group. I'd still fuck the singer though. Nice bum. We also

make friends with a local girl and her twat
of a boyfriend. She's cool so we put up with
the presence of her twat. We have a round of
arm-wrestles of which I am the victor of but
only just beating Johnny. I don't normally
like this kind of behaviour. I would never
raise this as an activity, I find it
socially primitive and it's usually alpha
nob heads that suggest it. The twat
boyfriend then tries to capitalise on this
and arm-wrestles Chris and Johnny after me
and to my surprise beats them and he looks
quite scrawny. But having just used their
energy trying to beat me I'm not surprised,
and for which he was more than likely
waiting for. I notice he didn't challenge me
though. He keeps calling Johnny, Ginger as
in Ginger Baker, because Johnny's ginger and
a drummer. He thinks this is amusing but I'm
just finding it rude and Johnny's smiling
but I'm fairly certain he wants to break the
guy's nose. We carry on partying and mostly
ignore him. When his girlfriend and I pop
out for a fag I give her a good old snog.
That'll learn him! Back in the bar someone
hands me the guitar and we have a good old
sing-song. I play one my old favourites
Hotel Yorba and it gets the whole bar going.
It's a great atmosphere and everyone's
getting involved and there are some very
pleasant, funny people in here. After the
bar closes we head to the square and carry
on playing there. By now it's around 3am and
any thoughts of taking it easy are long
past. We have a bit of crowd around us as we
play songs in the square and the party's
still going. As the crowd slowly disperses
we make our way back to the hostel but find
a bar that's still open around 4am. We rush
in there and buy some beers and climb on
some young peoples' table and start dancing

away. At first they look at us like we're deranged but they soon warm to the idea and they're up dancing with us. We have a couple of drinks but I can barely finish my second. We're all fucking steaming. We fall out of the pub and into the street where the sun is now making an appearance. I head off without the others on my own for some reason and after about 10 minutes I decide to take a rest and lay down in the middle of the road and take a nap. When I next open my eyes I see Andy, Chris and Johnny running down the road towards me with their cocks out. I am now awake.

That morning, none of us are feeling too clever. We've all got stinking hangovers and are struggling to wake up after about 3 hours sleep. We have to grab our gear and head down to the festival on a bus down in the valley. The organisers of the battle of bands are none too impressed with us, having heard of last night's antics and drunkenness. They obviously expected a lot more professionalism, but then, that's them buying into the importance of their own competition. It isn't important. It's fucking bullshit. No important competition has paid entry! It's not as if at the end of it you can win a contract with Sony. You win a few days in studio and a pat on the back. We just got lucky and raped it for what it is.

We're sitting back stage with half an hour to go and Chris is fast asleep sitting on the plastic furniture they've supplied. We get free beers and red bull, which we ply ourselves with beforehand. We need the energy. We meet the Maccabees whilst we're backstage as they're playing the same stage as us, which does add a bit more kudos to

the affair. At least we're playing on the
same stage as a decent band. They were, of
course, nothing to do with the competition.
We're called up to go on stage and I give
Chris a nudge and he awakes. We arrive on
stage in a rather languid fashion but we
give it our best shot. I felt like we played
a pretty good set and the other bands
watching seemed to like it and by this point
we'd gained ourselves a bit of a rock-n-roll
reputation in the camp. I felt we were doing
the Brits proud! The songs went down pretty
well with the crowd and we certainly enjoyed
the experience. We clamber off stage and
have our picture taken as all the bands do
after they have performed. At least we
looked like a fucking band. After we play,
some Norwegian metal band come on wearing
gas masks and nuclear-type suits. Fuck me!
Are they still pedalling this shit? Hasn't
that look been done a thousand times? The
Dutch band play and they are a decent
outfit. The girls are pretty cute and I've
got my eye on the little blonde bassist.
They are admittedly quite young but in all
honesty that's never been something that's
bothered me before. I don't consider age to
be much of problem so long as they are old
and mature enough to understand what they
are doing. Is that totally true. The
instinct/reptile brain part of me says I
would have sex with a 16yr old if she
pursued me and supposedly this has something
to do with our evolutionary history of
breeding. We would see the young as more
fertile and more likely to be a virgin and
so that leaves little doubt that the
offspring we produce is more likely to be
our own. But we are not animals and the
moral cognitive part of my brain box says
that's wrong, because they most likely don't

understand what they're doing and perhaps it could be psychologically damaging. In our society we are told that 16 is the legal age of consent and if you have sex with a 15 year old you're a paedophile. If a girl tells you she's 18 and you have sex with her and you later find out that she's 15, does that make you paedophile? Are you responsible? In the heat of the moment whilst they are unzipping your fly, it's unlikely that you're going to say, 'Hold on, can I see your driver's licence?'

I think the sexuality and maturity of girls differs from person to person. Some girls may feel like they want to be sexually active and are mature enough at 14, and some not until their early 20s. In some countries the age of consent is 12, which seems pretty terrible to me. When I see a 12-year-old or even some 18-year-olds, they look like children. If you think they look or act like children, then they probably are, so leave them alone. Sex really is my major vice in life, apart from some of that killing stuff, but they deserved it. Walking the line of what's right, what's wrong? Who gets hurt, who doesn't is a difficult one. Sex is a complicated area for example, many women fantasise about being raped but it doesn't mean they actually want to be. When I see a rape scene in a movie it deeply disturbs me, often for weeks after. I feel intense anger at the rapist and want to torture them and cut their dick off and choke them with it but at the same time, I'm also turned on by it. I digress.

The girls come off stage and we go and have a chat with them and watch a couple of the other bands together before heading off for a walk around the festival to go and have a look at the other stages. I would say there

was around 30,000 people or so camping here.
The rest of the bands in the competition
seem pretty shit and very pop and cheesy
rock. As it happens, the Japanese
representative band are pretty good. The
irony. They're pretty damn hot too. I sure
as hell didn't see *them* out last night. The
remaining bands are due to play tomorrow.
There's a band we catch later on from
Denmark that are very pop rock but good at
what they do if you like that kind of thing.
The lead singer is very confident and keeps
leaving the stage and running around and
gives one of the Japanese girls a kiss. It
is an impressive performance in terms of
entertainment and I hate him.
After the day's events we head back to the
hostel and meet up with the Dutch band at 12
Bar, the place we came to last night. The
beers are going down surprisingly well after
last night's debacle. We are having a good
laugh with the girls and Mary, the local
girl from last night, is back with the twat,
her boyfriend. I think he suspects that
something happened last night but can't
prove a thing. I just give him a big old
knowing smile. We hang out till about 4am
and I manage to steel a kiss from the Dutch
bass player. She's shy but later on we fuck
behind the pub. You just never know. 98.

Mary's boyfriend is doing my head in so when
he goes outside I follow him and tell him
I've got some coke if he wants some. He
agrees and follows me around the back of the
building. He goes first and I make sure no
one sees us. As he gets close to the wall I
smash his head into the stonework and he
drops with a thud. I undo his trousers and
pull them down a bit so it looks like he's
come out for a piss and slipped. He just

lays there with an expressionless look on his face and his small pale flaccid cock hanging out.
I go back and in and about half an hour later Mary asks if I've seen her boyfriend and I say that I haven't and that he must have gone home. He never had any money and she bought all his drinks. She shrugs and says, 'Oh well.' I do the same.
When we go back to the hostel to sleep the lads seem to have some sort of irritable bowel syndrome as the air in the room is thick with the smell of their arseholes. They're farting constantly and I can barely fucking breathe so I take my pillow and sleep in the cold barren corridor.
The next day, they read out the results at the festival and we end up coming something like 10th out of about 20 bands. Pretty shit. It was fairly clear that the Germans didn't really get our music and the organisers were still pissed at us for getting so rat-arsed. It was of course disappointing to do so badly but, fuck it hey. At least we put on a good show and enjoyed the experience.
Mary came to say goodbye to us when we left and said that she still hadn't seen her boyfriend and assumed that he had gone off in huff. She didn't seem that bothered so neither was I.
We said our goodbyes and jumped on the coach to the airport. The coach back was fairly quiet. I think there was a great deal of introspection occurring on that journey. It had been quite an experience for all of us. I suppose it was a minor glimpse into the world of professional musicians who get to do this stuff for a living and I must say it suits me very well.

x Curling x

What's the point?

x Peasants x

If there's one thing I cannot stand, it is
people honking their car horns at one
another when they have to wait for more than
two fucking seconds. It makes my blood boil.
I head out of my flat to visit a new client
I've acquired through a fuck buddy. They
want to talk to me about doing some
freelance footwear design, which is great
because the few shifts I did at The Finsbury
pub were draining the life out of me. It's
run by a pair of paranoid, controlling,
Turkish pricks who are constantly there. Not
working or helping, just watching. You can't
even have a drink. What's the point of
working in a bar if you can't even have a
couple beers whilst you slog your guts out
for the public's enjoyment?
I walk out and go to cross the road when
some bitch in a bright yellow Seat Ibiza
comes out of nowhere and nearly takes me out
and then blasts her horn at me. Fortunately
she stops before flattening me and I raise
my arms as if to say, 'What the fuck?'
This cunt gets out the car and with a
common, strong Essex accent starts shouting
shit at me.
'Oi, you fuckin' prick. Why don't ya look
where ya goin!! Are you fuckin' blind or
sominck? I nearly crashed me fuckin' car!!!'
She continues to rant and gets right up in
my face.
'Are you fucking kidding me, you moronic
peasant? This isn't a fucking motorway. You
need to fucking slow down.' I retort.
'Think you're better than me, do ya? Think
you're so fuckin' smart, do ya? I'll fuckin'
do you in, you posh prick. I'll….'

SMACK!!! I head-butt her square in the bridge of her nose and it explodes and there's blood all over the place and she hits the road like a dead fish. I see that we're drawing attention so I make a sharp exit and head down to Seven Sisters tube station whilst a small crowd gathers around the shocked and bewildered peasant bitch. I re-emerge at Swiss Cottage and using Google maps I navigate my way to the Marriott hotel. How did we ever find anything before? I head up to the lounge area and make myself a coffee. My client Vijay arrives and we get down to business. He has a factory in India and he wants to sell shoes in the UK but has no customers yet. I look at his current range and I can see why. He wants me to be honest and so I am.
'You need a whole new range if you want to appeal to the UK market.'
'Ok!' He agrees and we go to Oxford Street to buy some shoes to copy the last of.
'At some point you will have to come to India!' he says.
Fuck, I didn't think I'd be going back there again. The last time I was there I murdered a giant baby.
I've got a date tonight with a girl called Sparky. What a name! I met her on Tinder and she seems just enough on the good side of a bit mental and all I can tell about her appearance for sure is that she is slim and from her WhatsApp profile photo of her and her two friends sitting naked at the edge of a river with their backs to the camera is that she has a damn fine back and ass. Every photo of her is different so I've no idea what she really looks like and there's not one particular photo that's that convincing

that she's even attractive. She looks a bit
old in some of the photos but she's only 28.
I arrive to meet her at a nice old pub in
Angel, Islington, and she isn't there yet.
This isn't unusual. Girls often like to make
sure the guy is there first and I agree with
that. She walks in confidently and she does
indeed have an incredible ass. She's wearing
tight very dark grey jeans, a little black
top and leather jacket. She looks smart but
still with an element of cool and
individuality.

'Hi,' she says and we exchange kisses on the
cheek. Both cheeks because she's a bit posh
and because that's what they're like. She
buys the first round. A good sign!

The beginning of our conversation is a
little tricky, she is a little bit taller
than me and this knocks my confidence a bit
as I know and have been told on numerous
occasions that women prefer taller men. We
make some light conversation but I don't
feel all that comfortable and she seems
disinterested in what I have to say. Her
profession is upholstery and she seems quite
intelligent but soon realise that, that's
not the case and she's not such a bright
spark despite the name. The evening gets
better as it goes on, but not much.

Out of nowhere she tells me that,

'One of my friends called their child Bungle
because they liked Rainbow as a child.' She
is very amused by this story.

I replied by saying, 'I liked running around
and chasing my friends with dog dirt on the
end of a twig when I was a kid but I don't
have any intention of calling my future
child Shit-stick!' She laughs at my reply.
It's quite hard work and I am certain
nothing is going to come of this. Even when
I sense I'm in a losing situation I'm still

never the one to suggest leaving. Partly because I'm a pussy, partly because I'm getting to drink alcohol, and partly because, if there's still any possibility of a shag, I will stay, even if the building's on fire.
It gets to last orders and I say, 'One more?' and to my surprise she agrees.
We get into a conversation about Karma.
'I'm not really a great believer in it,' I say.
'Oh goddd!' She huffs putting her head on the table. 'What are you talking about maan' She's posh but has a hippy like side to her, as youths with rich parents can only really afford to be. One of those spiritual types which is another word for confused, pretentious and stupid. She has an all-over tan, blonde medium-length straight hair, and had worked on a ship doing a season of scuba diving, a season of snowboarding, you know the type. She's not interesting, though that never stopped me from wanting to fuck anyone before. It's terrible form, I know. I should be more selective, however this girl is very physically attractive. She has a pointy nose like a model. I think she may have said she's done modelling or at least told me that was her mum's profession. At this point I think I've blown it, but you have to draw the line somewhere so I stand by what I said.
'I can't believe in anything where so many bad things can happen to so many good people. Adolf Hitler got to kill himself. That's not Karma. Karma would be if he was raped by Jews for the rest of his life whilst watching them torture his friends, family, children and that dog he had. Okay, maybe not the dog.'

I'm not winning her over and fortunately the conversation turns to another subject, although I know I've lost her.
The barman rings the bell and that translates as, 'Fuck off home so we can too'.
'Fancy a nightcap?' she says.
What? I was not expecting that. I never really know what nightcap means. Does it mean just a late drink or does it always mean, 'do you want to screw'?

'But just for a drink,' she says.
Ah, so it is just a late drink.
'Yeah sure,' I say.
We buy 5 bottles of tonic water from the bar and head outdoors. Her front door is right next to the entrance to the pub. Perfect. It's an old-ish flat. Probably built in the 60s. We climb a flight of stairs to enter into it. There's a small open-plan kitchen/lounge with one of those stool seated type dividers. I think they call them breakfast bars? She cuts up some fresh lemon and squeezes them by hand into two large glasses of vodka and tops it up with tonic water and they're pretty damn good. I've already had about 4 pints of lager and with this on top I'm feeling a bit tipsy and much more confident than I was, especially now that she invited me back. It means that she at least likes something about me, or maybe she's just lonely. We down the first round of drinks with haste and she makes another. She's playing me some music on her Mac. She shows me some shite electro music but then surprises me by showing me a video of Coco Rosie and they are wonderful. It makes me look at her differently. It hints that deep down she does have good taste in some things. I have never heard them before but I

like it a lot. It's not often I find a new
band I like.
As we get more pissed we start dancing
around. I move in closer and try to steal a
kiss but she seems to be resisting so maybe
it was just for a drink. I go back in after
more dancing and this time she returns my
affection. We sit on the high stools and
continue snogging when we both lose our
balance and get thrown to the floor in a
very undignified fashion but when you're
this drunk you don't give a damn. I pick her
up and put her back on her stool both
laughing. After we've collected ourselves
the snogging resumes and she takes my hand
and places it on her right tit. Hmm, this
looks promising. I give her tits a good old
feel and they're a decent size for her
build. Then she pulls away, pulls down the
front of her stretchy tight jeans and starts
rubbing her pussy in front of me. I get off
my stool and move into her body with her
legs wide apart. I pick her up and take her
over to the seating. I pull down her jeans
and knickers in one go and quickly remove my
own. Not knickers. She then says, 'I can't,
I'm on my period.'
'I don't, care.' I shrug.
'I can't, I don't normally do this,' she
says. The amount of times I've heard that.
'I don't care,' I say again, 'Take it out.'
'Okay, one minute.' She replies.
She goes into the toilet and comes back out
minus a tampon. She tells me to fuck her
from behind. There's a shelf above a
redundant fireplace with a large mirror. She
places her hands on the shelf and stares at
herself as I slide my cock inside her.
There's no real sign of blood it must be
near the end. I start to fuck her slowly.
Her arse is even better in the flesh.

I fuck her long and deep but slow.
'Hit me,' she requests.
I pause for moment. I then grab my belt off the chair, pull it tight and give her a good old whack around her arse and she groans with pleasure. I hit her pretty hard the next time which makes her arse go red which kind of puts me off a bit so I chuck the belt away. I start fucking her faster whilst she also plays with her clit at the same time. The only slight problem is that because she is a bit taller than me I am having to stand on my tip toes which is making me tense my stomach and there's no chance I'm going cum like this. I persist as I am enjoying it nonetheless. After a good amount of shagging her from behind, I take hold of her and put her on her back on the cushioned flat surface against the wall. She looks fucking hot in this position. Slim, tanned, sun-kissed brown, blonde pubic hair (what there is of it), great tits and her legs are wide open waiting for me. Her pussy staring at me! Sometimes you just can't believe it. I almost feel guilty or like at any moment she's just going to say 'stop, I can't do this', but no she's still into it. We get going and I can feel already this was a smart decision and in about 5 minutes I pull out of her and cum all over her belly. She's not on the pill. It is surprising the amount of women that are willing to trust that you're not going to fill them with your baby-making juice. It's now about 4 in the morning and I'm well and truly bollocksed.
'Let's go to bed,' I say.
'You have to go home,' She says.
'No fucking way, it's late and I'm not paying for a cab, come on,' I say.
'You have to go.'

'No.' I tell her. I climb up the stairs and into her room and she only has a single bed. I de-robe and climb into her cold bed. She comes up stairs and says, 'I've only got a small bed.'
'So I see. Come on, it's fine.' I reply. I'm out like a light. In the morning I open one of my eyes tentatively and turn over and give her a spooning. She stirs a little. I feel the warmth of her smooth body against mine under the cover of the duvet. I put my arm around her body and my hand around her breast. She pushes back against me. I love this position and so I already have a hard on. I kiss her at the top of her back and the side of her neck and she makes long soft breaths. She reaches back and takes hold of my cock and starts to wank me. It's usually me badgering women for morning sex and they often aren't up for it when it's the first time.
Sparky guides my cock inside her with her hand. I like this a lot. This hot girl is actually pulling me inside her. It feels wonderful. You never know how someone is going to be in morning. We have slow sleepy spoon sex and it feels divine. After a while I roll her onto her front. I close her legs and lie on top of her and continue to fuck her from behind. I pretty much always cum in this position. She is playing with her clit whilst I fuck her and as soon she cums I allow myself to cum all over her magnificent arse.
I picture her arse for the whole of the next week. The image from when I was screwing her in front of the mirror made a lasting impression on my brain, which I really don't have space for. It's probably pushed out mathematics, simple language, or how to use the oven. It's ironic that when I was 17 I

vehemently believed one should be in love before they lost their virginity, but love seems hard to come by these days. 99.

x This Is The End x

It's not the end.
Following our frolicking in Germany we're
back in Blighty playing a gig at the o2
arena in Angel but in the smaller room. We
play a good show to an appreciative crowd
with a good few of our friends in tow and
it's the usual drunken behaviour. Jesse is
there and she has a new jet-black bob cut
and she's wearing red lip stick, and is
dressed in tight black denim and leather.
She looks hotter than ever but she kind of
hates me for fucking Izzie. After a few
drinks and jokes she loosens up and soon
enough we're snogging in the gents toilet
and before I know it my cocks in her smeared
red lipstick mouth.
I head out for a smoke and there's some guy
outside being a bit of a cunt. He turns out
to be a guy who owns a record label so I let
his derogatory comments about our music
slide for now. He says we're good but not
that good and could be better. He blabs on a
bit in a self-important manner that doesn't
impress me but I'm so desperate to make
something out of this music lark I'd listen
to the Teletubbies discuss quantum
mechanics. The guy is called Ell and he's a
spoilt white Iranian rich boy who has a flat
in Hampstead Heath courtesy of Daddykins.
We have a meeting with him the next day at a
pub in Primrose Hill and the things he's
promising sound too good to be true. He's
talking about investing 50 grand in the band
and paying for us to record an album. We
can't believe our ears, but that doesn't
mean he isn't a cunt.
He books us a few gigs over the following
weeks and all is going fairly well until we

have another meeting and Ell is being the
usual prick and is slagging us off so Andy
tells him he's going to knock him out. We
leave the meeting.

We all make up later and Ell comes round my
flat with everyone else for a bit of a get
together. He's sitting on my sofa with the
dog he's brought that's pretty big and
called Shy. We later consult on this but
we're all fairly certain that at some point
in the evening he was rubbing the dog's
vagina. When he falls asleep late into the
night we cover him in porno playing cards
and make up and take a few snaps. You never
know when they might come in handy.

A couple of weeks later and Ell has drafted
a contract for us to read, which states that
he takes all the rights to all of our songs.
We of course do not agree and we ask him to
draft a new contract and he refuses so we
tell him to fuck off. What once seemed like
a promising endeavour was now just a poo in
a box.

A few weeks later I contacted a few of the
recording studios that Ell informed us had
rejected us. There were studios such as the
one that recorded the Arctic Monkeys first
album that he claimed he could get us into.
The studio told me the reason they rejected
us was because Ell wanted to pay them 2k for
a project that costs 10k.

After this the band started to lose its way
a bit and I think we all felt quite
dispirited. At our next gig at Proud
Galleries in Camden, Andy announces, 'Lads,
this is going to be my last gig before we
end up not being mates anymore.'

I had been thinking of ending it myself for
a while and this came as a bit of a relief.
We all agreed then and there that this would

be our last ever gig. We gave each other a
hug and wished each other well for the gig.
When we staged I announced to the crowd,
'I'm afraid to say that this is going to be
the last gig for The Winter Kicks.'
The crowd or at least the group that know us
gasped and a few 'nooos' were shouted out
which felt good to hear.
'We want to thank all our friends who have
supported us on our journey these past few
years, it's been a blast. Now let's play
some fucking songs!'
I loved the band and all the fellas in it
and it's a shame nothing came of it but it
is hard work making a band that becomes
successful. There are loads of knock-backs,
waiting for hours to play your gig after
sound check. Lugging your instruments around
on the underground and on buses. Barely
getting paid if ever at all, sometimes
playing to a man and his dog. It's tough,
for sure. In my heart, I think the three of
them welcomed the end of the band with a
sigh of relief as it's easier to accept
defeat and give up than it is to keep
fighting knowing you may never win and in
that I think there was a sense of cowardice
in that. They all just gave up music
completely. Chris and Andy moved back to the
small town they grew up in and Johnny simply
put down his sticks never to play again.
There was no way that I was going to give up
on music, it means too much to me and I'm
sure somewhere in their hearts they'll feel
a small amount of regret in the future,
though I sincerely hope they do not. Perhaps
I'm foolish to pursue this dream but I have
to try, I have to. I shall miss them a great
deal. It has been the best 3 years of my
pointless existence. I love you all very

much and wish you well. Farewell 'my boys, my boys.'

x The Walk of Death x

It's not really a 'Walk of Death' but that's what Steph called it. I think since my Dad died and being sacked from my job and the band splitting up, she suspects I lost my mind slightly and that was the only reason I liked her. An element of that might well be true but as someone far wiser and more intelligent than me pointed out, how can the very organ (the brain) that is damaged, diagnose itself as being so. Does having the awareness that you might be losing your mind mean that you're not? You just think you are? Do mad people even recognise that they're mad? Surely that's what makes someone actually mad, the non-recognition of it? I really think they should bring back the interrobang!? It looks like a question mark but with a vertical line through it that is the exclamation mark so it's the combination of the two. It's perfect for sentences that are neither statements nor questions.

So, back to the 'walk of death'! Seeing as I currently have nothing going on in my life, no job, no band and no one whom I love and who loves me I thought, 'I need to get out into the wild and get some mountain air into my lungs. Get the fuck out of grey concrete, peasant-filled London for a bit.' I have been intending to go on a trek since I went on a walking holiday in Yorkshire a couple of years ago. It felt exhilarating standing on the tops of those lush green hills with no sign of human life other than an abandoned rusty old bath. I'm sitting staring at my mac, thinking right, where the fuck do I start? Hmmm… Hmmm…

Ah! I know lets just Google, the best hikes in the world. Up pops 'Top 20 Hikes in the world.' Perfect!
South America looks amazing but a bit too far and out of my current budget. Hawaii? I wasn't expecting that. Iceland looks good but it's fucking expensive. Ireland, nice but only a one-day hike, I want something a bit more challenging than that. Mont Blanc. Hmm, this one looks interesting. It reads:

'Mont Blanc is part of the Alps and has the highest mountain peak in Europe. It borders with France, Italy & Switzerland and the hike is 100 miles all the way around and takes between 8-12 days depending on your fitness and ability. Difficulty: Medium / Hard'

The photos of the hike look incredible. This looks like exactly what I'm after. I do some further investigation. You can book with a guide but it's much more expensive than just going alone and booking your own accommodation so I think I can bloody well do this on my own, how hard can it be? Though this thought is still tinged with a sense of trepidation. Looking at something on a map and thinking, 'Hey, that looks pretty easy,' and actually being there are two completely different things. It's similar to when you exit a tube station and you haven't got a clue which exit to leave from and you've got no internet connection so you just choose any exit using your gut instinct which is usually always the wrong one and then you walk for 10 minutes to discover you've gone in the wrong direction once you've got your internet connection back and Google maps is working again. If I can't even navigate my way out of a tube station successfully, I'm not likely to be

very capable of navigating around a mountain range with only a map and a compass. I've never even used a compass before. I shake that idea out of my head and get on with the task in hand. After 4 arduous hours of booking tiny wooden huts in the middle of nowhere in places that don't have email and you have to telephone them and they don't speak English, I have eventually booked my accommodation, flights, coaches and trains. Done!
Shit!
What am I doing?
Ah, it's fine.

The next step is to buy all the gear one requires for these kinds of excursions. Perhaps excursion might be a bit too grander a term for this *trip*. The first thing I need is some sturdy boots that won't fall apart or kill my feet. On researching hiking boots I discovered they don't do them in my size. Well, men's ones anyway as I'm a size 6, so I ended up buying ladies walking boots for my 'walk of death'. What a man! Surprisingly Sports Direct is really good for last season's hiking gear. I'm sure it's not the best gear available but if you go to a proper outdoor shop it costs the earth to fully kit yourself out. They even had a compass, a first aid kit and the most important item, a whistle. I can't say I find the whistle very reassuring. They have a whistle attached to life jackets for in the unlikely event your plane crashes. I don't like the term 'unlikely', I'd prefer the term 'definitely'. I also don't like it when the pilot announces that we really should listen to the safety instructions. I'm not a particularly fearful flyer but when the pilot announces that, you think,

'Why do I need to listen? What does he know that I don't? Is there a lightning storm ahead? Did the plane fail its MOT? Is he not feeling well? If we do crash into the middle of the Atlantic Ocean, the first thing that comes to mind as a solution is not a small plastic whistle. 'Toot. Tooot, toot. Why isn't anyone coming? I'm only 3,000 miles away from anywhere. Why can't anyone hear me? 'Toooot, tooooooooowoot!'
I already have a warm hat and gloves that I stole from Stream Creek. I ordered a map online and when it came I opened it up and it was bigger than a Subbuteo pitch. I can't be opening this massive fucker up on the top of a 60mph windy mountain. Oh, and good socks! You need good socks! I know I'm getting older because socks at Christmas are now actually a good present for me.

So the day has come for my departure and I must say I'm mildly shitting myself. These days I often get slightly anxious about travelling. One reason I get anxious about flying is that I once went to the airport one week too early and on another occasion I went to the wrong airport and missed my flight so now I don't trust myself anymore and have to check the airport, flight times, train times about 50 times before I leave home and on the way there. The second reason is whenever I go on a trip that's more than a few days I have a sense of impending doom that I'm never coming back and I always say farewell to Scout as though I'm never going to see her again. Last night I packed my rucksack for the duration of 11 days, which is pretty tough. I packed and re-packed 4 times, taking something out each time. I doubt I'll need so many condoms, for god's sake. I doubt I will need so many books. I

always take around 3 books when I travel and
I barely even get through one third of one
book.
This is my final check list:

- 3 pairs of pants and socks.
- 2 t-shirts
- 1 pair of jeans
- 1 pair of lightweight breathable
  trousers that turn into shorts.
  Genius!
- Hat & gloves
- First aid kit
- Oat chocolate bars
- Smoking equipment
- Passport
- Condoms x 3. Maybe a goat will be up
  for it.
- Compass
- Common Sense
- Water proofs
- Phone & charger.
- Boots
- Whistle. Don't forget the whistle!!

'Bye Scout! Scoout!! Scooout!!! Scout!! Come
here!'
Why does one's cat always hide when you're
trying to say your last goodbye!!
'Scout!'
Finally I get her in my arms and hold her
like a baby.
'Bye Scout, I love you. Jo and Harriett will
look after you. Tell me if either of them
interferes with you in any ungodly way,
okay! Okay, right, bye poppet socks.'
'Meeeoowww.' she says in what sounds like,
'Don't go!!!' It probably means, 'you better
not let me fucking starve to death you
selfish cunt or I'll shit on your pillow.'

Out the door I go with a massive backpack on that's almost the same size as me. Once I start to make the journey I instantly start to calm down. I've always had a fear of fear, and then when I do the thing that I'm fearful of I find I'm not afraid at all. Perhaps it's just an anxiety of some sort. I walk to Turnpike Lane to get the Piccadilly line that takes me an hour and a bit to get to Heathrow. 33 stops. It's only about an hour and half flight to Geneva, which goes smoothly and I don't have to use the whistle whilst being eaten by jellyfish (do jellyfish eat people?) in the middle of the ocean even though we didn't cross any oceans, only a sea (though technically it's all one ocean). From Geneva I ride a coach that takes me up into the Alps on the French side. After about 2 hours of travelling through mountainous winding roads we arrive at the shack I'm staying at. I jump off the coach and head into the small isolated wooden building at the top of the hill and it is completely empty. I wander around and there's no one to be seen so I sit down feeling like an idiot not quite sure what to do with myself. 1 hour later the warden appears who apparently has an afternoon sleep around this time. This is France, I suppose. They're not exactly known for their warm welcomes and customer satisfaction. He shows me to my bunk bed in a room that I discover I am sharing with 4 others. I ditch my rucksack and take a walk to the nearest town, which is just over an hours walk away. It's a pretty town and it's a lovely sunny day so I have a slow walk around the place. I see a really pretty girl busking on the cobbled streets. She's playing her own songs on a harmonium. She is attractive and very talented and it pretty much breaks my heart.

When you see someone that you just know you would get along with but there's nothing you can or will do about it. I find a chair at the café/bar opposite from where she is playing and watch her for a while. After a couple of large glasses of nice cold French lager I feel a bit tipsy. Eventually I pluck up the courage to talk to her.
'Hi!' I say.
'Hi!' she replies.
'Where are you from?'
'Brighton but I have been travelling around France busking for three months, but I go home tomorrow.'
Bollocks!
'What brings you here?' she enquires.
'I'm doing the Mont Blanc trail. Do you play around London?'
'No, not really, I don't like London.'
Fair enough, I think. I kind of like her for saying that, and in a non-pretentious or ignorant sounding way. I've always thought London was a wonderful place but I'm having my doubts these days. I have tired of it somewhat.
'Well, it was nice meeting you.' I say, sensing that she might want me to fuck off so she can pack up and go.
'Yeah you too, enjoy the tour.'
A massive depression kicks in and I feel like I just lost something very important to me. It doesn't happen very often but very occasionally you meet someone that you just feel you could really connect with in a very pure sense and then you have to watch them walk away knowing you will never see them again, and you will never know if that was the person you'd been looking for all this time. It hurts. It's the not knowing that hurts the most I think. All this time I'd liked the idea of having a musical

girlfriend. I don't mean like a doll that you pull the cord of and she sings, 'She'll be coming round the mountain when she comes…'.

It seems that it would make sense to date a musician, alas, it's never happened. I've played music for years and not one musical girlfriend, well, apart from Xan but she wasn't an active musician anymore, she was a classically trained musician and that type of music can drill the fun out of it sometimes, especially if your parents forced you into it.

I stand around for a minute pondering on what could have been. I know it's a sad state of affairs and I shouldn't read too much into it but sometimes you just know. But then maybe I don't know. I've been wrong about almost everything before. I catch a bus back to the area I'm staying in. I get off at the wrong stop so I have to walk a bit further than anticipated and I realise that it's quickly getting dark and my shack is somewhere at the top of a hill and I don't think I can remember where it is. I decide to take a short cut through the woods, which only worsens the situation. Fuck, which direction is it? Well, I know its up, so I head in that direction. I finally clamber out of the woods up a steep hill and I'm out of breath and there it is, right in front me. Thank the lord. There's a couple sitting outside the hut drinking red wine. The lady is in her early thirties and he is about 50 and is white with dreadlocks. It's a bit of an out-dated look, but each to their own. I go inside and ask for some wine also and go out to join them and roll a cigarette. The warden comes out to join us and to have smoke. He starts to tell us about the last time he ascended up the mountain I'm going up tomorrow and that he watched some guy walking along a narrow ridge there and suddenly slip and fall out of sight. Great! That's just what I wanted to hear. I have couple more glasses of wine knowing I'll never get to sleep stone sober sharing a room with complete strangers and snoring men. I climb up the wooden stairs and unroll my sleeping bag, take off my clothes apart from my pants and after a short while feeling a bit pissed I slip into unconsciousness.

In the morning I don't want to mess around, so I get dressed, clean my teeth and pack up some lunch consisting of bread and cheese, which is the only option available. I down a couple of cups of coffee, there's no point in even attempting to make a good cup of tea. Just go with what's local is what I've learnt from my travels. Don't try and anglicise everything. I pack up my rucksack, put my boots on and get myself out onto the road thinking, 'Actually, where the hell does this trail start?' I walk towards a very small town where I'm informed by the warden I should head towards. When I get there I open up my guidebook to try and locate an access point to the trail. I'm walking along the only street through the town and I see some other hikers. I don't want to ask, but I think I've been walking on this road for 20 minutes now and I haven't really got a clue. I approach a couple and say, 'Hi, do you know where start of the trail is?'

'Yeah, its behind you.'

Now I feel like a complete tit.

'Ah, thanks.'

The couple are a pair of Kiwis, not literally. The guy is a bit of a pumped up prat who clearly does this kind of thing all the time and is the kind of gimp who can't wait to give advice to someone who is a novice. He is a reasonably attractive guy but still a massive control freak / geek and his less attractive plump girlfriend looks as though she'd rather repeatedly punch herself in the cunt than be on this hike. My guess is that she didn't think she could ever bag a guy this good-looking and now she has to do anything he wants to keep him happy. A hot cool bird just wouldn't put up his kind of flannel. Poor cow.

I start the ascent up a rather steep hill and I instantly feel relaxed and happy that I'm now on the right track and have finally started my hiking adventure. It dawns on me quite soon that walking at an acute angle in the up direction for even 5 minutes is pretty knackering, and I'm well aware that this is barely the beginning. Virtually the whole of today is an ascent. One thing I will say for myself though is I'm determined and I don't give up easily. Soon enough my stamina starts to kick in and I'm really enjoying the burning and the feeling of my muscles working in my legs. I feel like a man for once in my life. I rarely do. I usually feel like a child that's been told they are an adult and given a load of responsibilities and just waiting for someone to say, 'Hahaha, we were only kidding. You are a child, you spoon-faced tit. Give us that job, those clothes and your flat back, and GO HOME TO YOUR MOTHER!!'

The sun is beating down hard and I'm sweating like 38 members of a Fat Club stuck in a coach in the middle of Egypt with all the windows closed and the heaters on full blast at the sun's peak hour. The first rule

of Fat Club is you don't talk about Fat Club! That's why I'm not in it! After an hour, I've lost anyone that was behind or in front of me. I come to a junction of sorts and looking at my map I'm not sure which way I'm supposed to go. Using my gut instinct, which is usually a mistake, I make a gut decision. Half an hour later I realise I've made a mistake and I've lost the trail. I see a singular house nearby and I walk towards it. The lady owner is outside with her Labrador. Classic dog! Good all-rounder, a bit like a Ford Mondeo. Yeah, yeah, I know, get out of the 90's.
'Hi, can you please help me? I'm lost.'
'Hi, no problem my husband is a retired guide he can help you.' Result!
The elderly gentleman who is in good shape comes out and takes my map and says 'Well, this map is wrong. They changed the route and didn't update your map.'
Brilliant!
'What I would do if I was you, is take your map, fold it up, put it in your bag and never look at it again. The trail is about 10 minutes up the road. From there just look for red markings that lead the way and you should be fine.'
'Thanks very much, I really appreciate your help.'
'No problem, good luck and don't forget to look up and enjoy the scenery, sometimes one gets caught up in the challenge and forgets why they are here and where they are.'
A fine point, sir! What a pleasant gentleman.

True to his word, in exactly 10 minutes I come to a red-marked post pointing back up the mountain with a list of a few destinations and their distance in kilometres. My destination is 20km away. I'm feeling good about being back on the track, though not a great start. The sun is still damn hot and I'm starting to get through my water and regretting that I didn't bring more. A couple more hours pass and this virtual constant ascent is becoming hard work. I notice there is one particularly steep section ahead, which I can see a group of people struggling to ascend, some more than others. It's not so steep you have climb or anything but it's still quite a challenge. I could do with a refuel so I use this as a mental reward to get myself up this section. I start with a reasonable pace and soon start to catch up to the older and fatter hikers at the back. The fatter ones are perspiring heavily and they look like someone has threaded a steel hook into their anus that's attached to some invisible wire and from the bottom of the hill a rotating machine is trying to pull them back down. One guy stops, stands up straight and then arches his back, lifts his chin skywards, mouth wide open and gasping for air and energy with tears of sweat rolling down his face. On the subject of anuses, I had a dream recently where I felt there was something wrong with mine. I was doing too many poos. Most of them could hardly be described as poo at least not in a solid form. Temporarily I get a job working in a guitar shop. In my lunch break I go into a warm wooden room at the back of the shop where I take a short but sharp wooden handled knife and starting at the top of my forehead I insert the knife just deep enough to reach my skull. I then draw the knife slowly down my forehead, in-between my eyes, across my nose and continue down my throat,

chest and stomach feeling my skin starting
to peel apart. Not breaking the line I
continue to cut right down past my genitals
and along my perineum where I then have to
put my hand behind my back to somehow pull
the knife all way up my bum crack and going
around my anus. I continue somehow up the
length of my back to my neck and then all
the way round the back of my head until I
eventually meet at the front of my forehead
where I started. On completing a 360-degree
incision I peel my skin off revealing a
gooey skeleton that still has pasty white
skin and hair left attached to my legs and
lovely little toes. I take hold of my
recently removed hide and hang it on a rusty
old steel blunt hook hanging from the
ceiling. It's damn hot in the back room and
my hide soon dries out into a leathery brown
and yellow state. I then consult a co-worker
and guitarist named Rab. Rab has a fine
moustache and looks like an American hick,
but in a cool 70's musician type way.
I ask Rab to shine a torch through the hole
where my anus is on my dried-out skin which
is still hanging from the hook, to see if
there are any additional perforations that
should not be there, thus causing my anus to
leak and piss out watery shit streams. Rab
stretches my skin out to expose my anus and
shines the torch right through it and the
dust seemingly takes a brief rest on the
rays of light streaming through my bottom
hole.
'Well, it looks okay to me. No sign of any
extra holes my man,' Rab illustrates.
'Ah, okay… Rab! How many poos do you do a
day?'
'Hmm, around three,' He coolly replies.
'Ah right! I'm the same.' And I feel a great
relief that there's nothing wrong with my

anus although I am now unsure how I am to
re-fit my dried out skin to my body.
I wake up. Relieved to have full skin
coverage and equipped with my anus in
perfect working order.

I pass a couple of young men in their early
20s and aim for the more elite of the group.
I want to be the first to the top. Up with
the best of them is a lady of around 55
years, fit as a fiddle and adorning a pair
of hiking polls. She has a strong, steady
and unrelenting constant pace and I'm
starting to loose the energy I had around 30
metres ago and determined not to beaten by
this, I suspect, German lady. I'm so damn
hot and in need of a drink of water. I push
on and increase my speed and soon enough I'm
getting ahead of the bitch. 10 metres to go
and I can see the brow and soon the view
beyond into a giant pine-tree-filled, rocky
valley. Which makes me gasp in wonder,
exhaustion and fear. I always imagine myself
falling whenever I experience great heights.
I stand at the top with my hands on my hips
like a real adventuring twat should, just
admiring the view whilst I catch my breath.
It's a cliché I know but it's absolutely
true. You feel so small and insignificant
amongst such grand wilderness and landscape.
It's not a melancholic or lonely feeling,
it's one of feeling connected to the earth
and that it is what we were created from and
knowing that one day we will return to it to
be reunited and recycled back into its very
soul. We shall be absorbed back into the
rocks and earth and exhaled back out by the
trees into the atmosphere, morphing into gas
or vapour, or maybe even converted into dust
lightly resting on the light beams shining

through someone's dried out anus in the back room of a guitar shop in Denmark Street.

I find myself a rock to sit on in the shade to cool down and take a big gulp of that very marvellous H_2O. Sometimes it's just the best thing there is. I retrieve a big old ham and cheese baguette I made back at the hut and it tastes fucking fantastic. I loooove sandwiches. I think it's fair to say that I like more sandwiches than I do people. Can you think of many people that are better than a sandwich? The other hikers arrive at the top out of breath and possibly suffering from heatstroke. Which is fun to watch whilst you eat a sandwich.

Well, I still have a long way to go so I take another swig of water and begin the next section of the day's hike. I get to enjoy some downhill and level walking ground for a couple hours before I reach another large hill. I never know what to call them. Is it just called a hill on a mountain or am I just on a hill on another really big hill or is it just a part of the mountain. Who cares! It's in the 'up' direction, that's all that matters. Half-way up I feel quite worn out and my water is starting to run out and I've still got another 5 kilometres before I reach the hut I am lodging in. I am really struggling to get up this damn hill and starting to get angry. I push on and seeing a couple of people nearing the top I use that for a bit of drive. Once I get to the top I virtually flop down onto the ground and drink what's left of my water. It's around 4pm but the sun is still burning my face. After I have collected myself I begin to descend but now my legs are fucked. Going down hill is proving to be just as hard on your legs as going up. I continue a sharp decline for an hour, which is hammering my knees. I cross a small wooden bridge over a stream once I hit flat ground, which feels so good. FLAT GROUND!! I LOVE FLAT GROUND!! Right now I love flat ground as much as sandwiches. I re-fill my water but I can sense I'm deeply dehydrated and my muscles are tightening up in my calves and thighs. I look up and see I have a shorter but much steeper climb ahead. It is only 95 meters up which doesn't sound like much but after you've been walking for 8 hours and it's pretty much vertical, it's a real killer. I am hot and irritated and I have to stop 3 times to catch my breath. Come on; keep going, nearly there. I can't remember ever feeling this worn out and fatigued. I'm now climbing on my hands and knees as it gets steeper and steeper and I virtually crawl the last few metres to the top. Thank the lord. Or whoever. Thank onion gravy; it's just as inane. After 5 minutes lying down I stand up to discover that I have got extreme cramp in both legs. I try to stretch my legs forwards but it gives me cramp in the back of my legs. I try to stretch backwards but it gives me cramp in the front of my legs. All I can do is stand perfectly still and it's bearable but of course I can't just stand here like one of those silver statue twats you find in Covent Garden. Each step is quite painful as I feel the cramp moving from the front to the back of my legs. I walk carefully, now feeling every rock and stone under my feet as my whole body is feeling sensitive. Fortunately the sun's heat has faded and is dropping quite fast. After another few hundred metres I see the hut I am staying in. Yes! At least I hope it's the hut I'm staying in. If it

isn't I'm staying there anyway. I arrive at
the small stone building with a wooden roof.
A shy young French girl welcomes me and
shows me to my dormitory where I will be
sharing with 8 strangers. This is the part
I'm not so keen on. I chuck my stuff on the
bed and go back to observe the sunset. It
really it is one of the most beautiful
things I have ever seen. I can see snow
topped mountains, glaziers, forests and
great plummeting valleys with the burnt
orange and fiery red hues of the descending
sun's rays decorating the mountain and trees
extremities. We are also surrounded by about
30 behemoth cows, all adorned with metal
bells strapped around their necks, creating
this constant clanging sound that's like an
out of time, drunk orchestra. Dinner is
served at 8pm and as you can imagine there's
not exactly a menu.

8 of us sit in a quaint stone-walled but
warm room heated by a wood fire. I used to
be a very fussy eater but as I've got older
I'm much better and I'm so tired and worn
out I'd eat the man's dick who's sitting
opposite me right now. For starters we are
served soup and bread, which is delightful.
There's little to no talk amongst the group
and what talk there is, is tedious and
small. Me being the only English person at
the table, I am not included in the
conversation in what mostly seems to be
German and Austrian and that suits me just
fine. I wasn't sure there would be, but yes,
yes, yes, yes, yes, yes, yes yesss!!! They
have booze!! Red wine!! Wooooww!! I'm
trying to control myself and not simply wolf
the glass down like a crazed vampire but
man; this is just what the doctor ordered.
For the main we have pan-fried potatoes,
some veggies and also some grilled beef (I

wonder if it's the cousin of one of the cows outside?). It's delicious. In a normal situation it's probably very average food and not particularly satisfying however in this scenario it's like a 3 Michelin-starred restaurant. I see the French girl is accompanied by her boyfriend, which is disappointing and makes me feel a bit depressed. It seems odd, such a young couple all the way up here in the middle of nowhere running this tiny place with nothing but a bovine orchestra for company. I bet they have really loud sex during the day when the place is empty. I bet they fuck on the wooden tables outside in front of the cows that are licking their lips and shitting themselves whilst the young French lad is banging the French girl's sweet young pussy! I WANT A FUCK, goddamnit. Hmmm… don't get depressed. What the hell is wrong with me? People think they can go travelling and expect something to change in themselves. Most people don't change whatsoever; they just take their problems with them and come back with them. A lot of boring people go travelling because they don't have a personality and they think that when they come back home with all these exciting adventures in their back pocket and all those riveting stories to tell their friends, at last *they* will, in fact, be interesting, AND funny AND wondrous AND a deep thinker AND enlightened AND attractive to the opposite sex AND admired by…… but… ah… oh… but… oh…ah…but…no…but!
But yes, unfortunately you're still a boring cunt, except now you've got a heightened sense of self-importance, delusions of grandeur and loads of audible opinions that you're sure are really important and impressive and worldly, though you don't

really quite know what they mean but it does sound like the kind of thing someone that is worldly and interesting would say… wouldn't they???? Pleaaase!!! Wouldn't they???!!

The dessert is fruit. Fuck that. There's fruit in the wine, more of that please. I roll a cigarette and go outside to have a smoke. Now that the sun has gone down, it feels quite cold and eerie as the mist rises around us covering the cow orchestra from sight, though their clanging is still audible though now less enthusiastic as if the booze is wearing off, like a tired old piano player in an old Irish pub after time has been called. I suddenly feel how alone we are out here and how far we are away from any civilisation, or telephones, or slags. Hikers tend to be pretty boring people. They are all fast asleep by 9pm and they don't tend to drink either, which does leave more for me. After a few more glasses of red wine I am truly knackered and wonder how my legs are going to fare tomorrow. I feel part idiot and part wimp. I creep into the room where some of the fuck pigs are already snoring and quietly climb fully clothed into my sleeping bag with some strange man's face breathing directly into mine on both sides of me. Ace! Fortunately I'm so tired I soon fall asleep.

Morning arrives like a fart in a bag. I can't wait to get out of this room. My legs feel fine which is a great relief. I've learnt my lesson on the water front and fill up two big bottles. I slip on my boots, which is a wonderful and comforting feeling that is the mental trigger that I'll be adventuring once again. It's exciting, not knowing what I'm going to see today, where I will go, how I might feel. A quick breakfast and lunch made for the day. I set off down a dry muddy and stony track that soon leads me to a forest of pines and other trees I don't know the name of. I really enjoy walking in the woods. I think I'd enjoy being a tree. Whenever I go into the woods I feel excited and am reminded of historical events and films that involve running and jumping and climbing and a bit more running and fighting and throwing and flinging and fighting again and then, 'I see you,' and then more running again and then more throwing again and a run jump swim thing and then running, again the running. Mmmm… woods. I'm really enjoying this part of the hike I could do just this all day long and it's not scary in the woods because you can't see the edge of the drop or at least you're a long way from it and the trees will look after you. After around 2 hours the path becomes smaller and smaller and I'm being pushed out towards the edge by the mountain. How rude. I don't enjoy the edge (or that guy in U2, what twattish name) and try to avoid looking into what is now a sheer drop. Scary. I'm losing my nerve as the path is now around 1 foot wide and about 2 feet from the edge and I'm well aware that there is no else around me for a quite some distance. The path then disappears and I am now faced with nothing but a section of a rock face 30 feet in length with only a metal chain attached horizontally along it. You've got to be fucking kidding me!? Fuck off, I'm not traversing that. One slip and I'm a fucking pancake. Fuck, fuck, fuck. I can't fucking go back. Come on man. Pull yourself together. Okay, one step at a time. Don't look down. All the usual shit that everyone says in every film like this. I take a grip on the chain. I find reassurance in the knowledge that I have the strength to hold my own body weight should I slip. I slowly move across, holding on for dear life and shaking like a leaf. What seems like an hour later and I'm back onto solid ground although the path is still very narrow. The route leads upwards and starts veering back to my relief away from the edge. That was stressful. I'm glad I did it and didn't let myself down. It really makes me hate myself being such a coward. After a couple more hours I reach a fork in the path. I stand and stare at it for a while. There's no clear indication of which one I should take? Hmm…the problem is that walking in the wrong direction can sometimes take an hour or so before you know for sure if you have. I make my decision and go right heading in the preferred direction of down. I walk for around 20 minutes and I am still none the wiser so I continue on. 1 hour later and still there is nothing to suggest I am going the correct way. There are no markings I can see although you can often walk for an hour without seeing a sign of any sort so that's not unusual. Do I continue and risk getting further from the track, or do I cut my losses and go back and try the other route? Shit! I'm feeling a bit foolish and starting to worry now. What should I do? Also, time is now against me as I know it's at least 3 hours to the next hut and I will die out here if I have to navigate in the dark or damn well freeze to death. If I run I can make up the time and reduce the time risk. I will be knackered but it's worth the risk. I decide to continue down the same path as it is down hill and so I will use less energy. I start to make some good amount of ground quite quickly though I still don't see any signs. As I am running down the side of the mountain I catch a glimpse of something that looks to be a red marking of some kind. I turn my head to look and my right foot catches on a tree root and I am flung forward and I can feel a weightlessness and an overwhelming sense of dread surging through my bones and my blood into my stomach. My body turns as I am falling but I don't hit the ground. I am still falling and now I see the edge of the path moving away from me as I fall into the valley and…

I feel a great pain in the back of my head and my ribs feels as though they are being crushed inside my body. I open my eyes and can see the edge leaning away from me. My ears are ringing loudly and I feel blood trickling out of them and down my neck as I try to sit up. I pull myself up to a sitting position and rest next to a large rock. I look up again at the ledge to ascertain whether it is surmountable. I must have fallen around 25 or 30 feet and I cannot see any potential route up nor down. The ledge I'm on broke my fall but it seems to be a cruel joke that is just prolonging the inevitable. I try to stand but I cannot. So I slump back down. I reach for my rucksack to retrieve my water bottle. Everything in my body hurts and it is starting to get dark now. I sit slumped against the rock and sip some water, which I feel lining my dried-out oesophagus like the first mountain spring through a dried out river. I must have been out for around two hours. Hanging out of one of my jacket pockets is the faithful bright orange plastic whistle. I retrieve the whistle. I feel out of breath as my ribs tighten around my lungs. I look at the whistle for a minute and smile. I toss the whistle over the edge and watch it tumble down amongst the vicious looking rocks and into their jaws that look like alligators teeth in wait of their meal. I see the sun slowly falling behind the mountains in the distance and watch the shadows grow and fill the valley with darkness as if putting the forest to bed. It's beautiful and for the first time, probably in my whole life I'm not afraid of anything. I think this is precisely where I'm supposed to be. I had my chance at life and failed miserably in all aspects. I have hurt many people, both physically and emotionally. I can hurt no one else here. I am bored of life and I am tired of being afraid, disappointed and constantly on the precipice of depression, melancholy and my unfading desire for cheap sexual satisfaction. I truly hoped I would find someone that I loved. That and my failure as a musician are my only true regrets. I had my chances to be loved but I threw them away. I really thought it was the right thing to do. I took a risk by holding out for what I thought I really wanted and whom I wanted to love, and well, it just didn't pay off. I don't regret that though. I lived by that motto and I still believe in it now, though I wish that just for a short period of my life I could have experienced real, true and honest love that felt like it would last forever. The kind you see in movies and read in books. I can imagine exactly how it might feel and I wanted it so very much.

It is getting colder by the minute and I am feeling very tired. I wrap my coat around me and put my hat and gloves on with some painful effort. There is a still a small afterglow of sunlight clinging on to what remains of the day. My eyelids are becoming heavy and I feel increasingly tired, calm and peaceful. I must sleep now. I do not know if I will wake in the morning, but I do not mind if I don't…

I never did get to 100!

The End

Note:

This is a work of fiction. Names, characters, businesses, places, events, locales, and incidents are either the products of the author's imagination or used in a fictitious manner. Any resemblance to actual persons, living or dead, or actual events is purely coincidental.

Printed in Poland
by Amazon Fulfillment
Poland Sp. z o.o., Wrocław